Research & Writing

Activities That Explore Family History

Written by Douglas M. Rife

Illustrated by Judy Hierstein

Teaching & Learning Company

1204 Buchanan St., P.O. Box 10

Carthage, IL 62321-0010

This book belongs to

Dedication
For my children, Aliya, Zain and Sofia

Acknowledgments
I would like to thank the following people for their contributions to this book:

Rachel Obermiller for permission to reprint excerpts from
Charles Monroe Staley's diary.

Pearl Johnson for permission to reprint excerpts from her book
Glimpses from the Past. Thanks also for pictures of the Vincent family.

And thanks to Shirley Rife, Myrtle Brooks and Gladys Kuelher
for use of their pictures and family information.

Originally published as *A Family History Handbook*.

Editor: Todd Sharp

Cover designer Sara King

Copyright © 2002, Teaching & Learning Company

ISBN No. 1-57310-360-8

Printing No. 987654321

Teaching & Learning Company
1204 Buchanan St., P.O. Box 10
Carthage, IL 62321-0010

Table of Contents

Dear Teacher or Parent,

This is not a how-to book for those searching their family histories but rather a writing activities book linked to the topic of family history. Most writing teachers instruct their students to write about "what they know." Often, students do not see the value or drama in writing about themselves or their families. But with practice and specific activities, students can work with members of their families to uncover the dramatic stories found in each family.

Special Note for Teachers

For the adopted student or for those who belong to blended or single-parent households, the search by "blood" may be painful or even impossible. When using writing activities in this book, please be sensitive to student concerns regarding privacy and family issues. While writing activities that students can share with their parents can be a great bridge from school to home, be mindful that some activities may not be appropriate as a part of your classroom discussion. If the situation does arise in which a student is unable to trace his or her ancestry through the biological parents, it should be emphasized to him or her that a search through one's adoptive or step-parents can be equally as valuable. Explain that the students' quests will begin and end with the people who love them most and whether DNA is involved or not, what they will discover will help explain how they came to be who they are and why. And that is, essentially, the reason we explore our family history in the first place.

Sincerely,

Douglas M. Rife

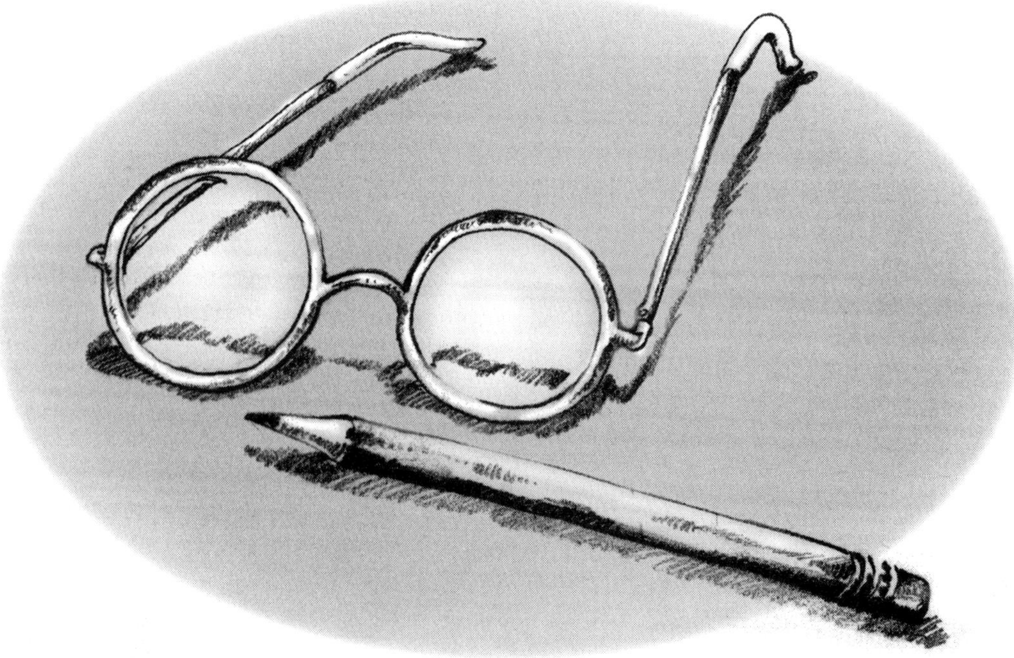

Introduction

Research & Writing
Activities That Explore Family History

Broad-streeted Richmond . . .
The trees in the streets are old trees
used to living with people,
Family trees that remember your
grandfather's name.

In this passage from *John Brown's Body*, Stephen Vincent Benet paints with a broad brush. He provides a sweeping description of Richmond, old Richmond, with old family names. These names span generations, back into the antebellum South. A sense of permanence fills the stanza. Family names endure.

Although Benet is not talking about "family trees" in the genealogical sense, we still get a feeling of family history. Even if a family's history cannot be traced back to the antebellum South, each family has a unique story, an individual experience, with a cast of players not duplicated by any other family. In this book, each student will search for his or her family's version of that story.

Following is a brief summary of the content and sequence of *Research & Writing: Activities That Explore Family History.*

Families: helps students learn how families are defined, and explains terms commonly used in family documents.

Family Relationships: starts students on their journey backward by explaining various types of family relationships. Exercises in this section are designed to help students understand how they relate to other members of their family.

Pedigree: gives students an idea of what family history charts look like. Students also become acquainted with accepted guidelines for filling in these charts.

Family Records: explains the importance of family records by concentrating on family Bibles and funeral programs as important sources of information.

Photographs: shows students how they can pick up clues about their family's past from photographs. Special attention is given to showing how photographs can trigger memories of family members.

Oral History: take a step-by-step approach to teaching good interviewing techniques, describing the difference between open and closed questions. This section leads the student through an interview with an immigrant from Norway, demonstrating the richness of family folklore.

The Internet: discusses how the emergence of the internet has revolutionized the speed and ease with which the family historian can find and retrieve family history documents.

Religious Records: gives a brief account of church history in this country and lists several church archives as sources for family history research. This section explains the types of records that can be found in churches and church archives.

Diaries & Journals: concentrates on a journal written in 1870 to reveal the importance of diaries and journals to family history. Students get a glimpse of rural life more than a hundred years ago and gain a feeling for the historical significance of diaries and journals.

Cemeteries: explains the wealth of family information found in cemeteries. The symbolism of gravestones and the importance of epitaphs are examined in detail. This section gives the students a chance to look at some of the more common gravestone symbols and explains how to do a gravestone rubbing.

Census Records: covers the history of the census, detailing the information that can be gleaned from United States census records. There is a description of the various censuses taken in the United States between 1790 and 1900.

Immigration: briefly explains the history of immigration. This section also tells students where they can find immigration records and passenger lists of ships that carried immigrants.

Maps: explains the growth of the United States. This chapter also emphasizes the importance of sound map-reading skills.

Wills: breaks down the legal jargon that students will have to wade through to understand wills and probate records. Students examine an actual will written in 1881.

Heraldry: discusses a part of family history that has evolved from the Middle Ages. Included is a brief history of heraldry and an explanation of the elements in a coat of arms.

Vital Statistics: introduces students to birth, marriage and death records. Students learn where these records can be obtained and how they can be used in family history research.

Newspapers: covers the information that family historians can find in newspapers. Special attention is given to obituaries and birth and wedding announcements.

Military Service: outlines the military records that are rich in family history information. In this section, students see actual military records from the War of 1812 and the Civil War.

	Objectives	Critical Thinking	Activities
Families	Define the term *family*.	Compare and contrast different views of the "family."	Draw a family pictogram.
Family Relationships	Introduce commonly used terms in family history research.	What makes me "me"? Where do I come from?	Investigate immediate family history.
Pedigree	Understand standard family history forms. – family worksheet – radial pedigree chart Develop a multi-tier time line.	Use a variety of resource materials to gather information. Transfer collected information into a time line.	Construct a pedigree chart.
Family Records	Introduce different sources of family information. – family Bibles – funeral programs – baby announcements – letters – city & county histories	What do these resources tell me about the people in my family? What kind of people were/are they? Personalities? Values? Life-styles?	Search city records. Search for old family letters. Have students find their own records to examine and react to.
Religious Records	Introduce religious organization as a source of records and documentation.	What do the records kept in churches tell me about my family? About the origins of my family? Values? History? Changes?	Find church records. Find family religious background over several generations.

	Objectives	Critical Thinking	Activities
Diaries & Journals	Introduce diaries and journals as sources of family history. Demonstrate writing style.	Analyze entries from a 19th century diary. Why are writing styles from the past different from today?	Journal for seven days.
Cemeteries	Understand cemetery symbolism. Understand the epitaph as a form of poetry.	Analyze gravestones for symbolism. Compare gravestone symbols.	Make a gravestone rubbing. Take symbolism test. Collect 10 samples of epitaphs. Create a unique epitaph.
Census Records	Understand the history of censuses and constitutional reasons behind the census. Identify the different family information to be gleaned from census records.	Analyze census schedules from 1790–1910. Compare to information from latest census.	Collect census data. Summarize data. Restate information in a summary chart. Conduct a neighborhood or classroom census.
Photographs	Introduce photos as a primary resource. Understand how culture and history can be interpreted from photos. Use family photos as a springboard for historical stories.	Analyze family photographs. Draw clues from family photographs. What can you learn about family members and the culture of the era from the photos?	Compare/contrast hairstyles and clothing from early 20th century photos to today's styles. Collect photos from the last century to the present.

	Objectives	*Critical Thinking*	*Activities*
Immigration	Explain commonly used terms. Identify sources for searching immigration records and passenger lists. Identify some key reasons for settlement in the U.S.	What reasons would people have for emigrating? How has immigration changed the "face" of America? Your family history?	Explore your family's immigration history OR explore the effect of immigration on your family OR the migration of your family across the U.S.
Maps	Reinforce map-reading skills. Understand the growth of the U.S.	Why did the U.S. expand? How was expansion accomplished? How are immigration and expansion connected? Explore the effects of immigration and expansion.	Research the major territory acqusitions after 1776 OR trace the routes of westward expansion. Find family records of migration.
Oral History	Understand the difference between open and closed questioning. Explain interview techniques. Review recording tips. Understand value of oral history.	Develop open-ended interview questions. Identify props to get the interview started. Explore advantages of human interaction over written accounts.	Interview a family member. Prepare a video or audio recording of the interview. Write a story based on information from the interview.
Wills	Introduce commonly used terms used in wills and probate records. Identify family history information that can be found in wills and probate records.	Analyze two wills for information.	Examine a will and answer questions. Write an imaginary will.

	Objectives	*Critical Thinking*	*Activities*
Heraldry	Introduce commonly used heraldry terms. Understand the historical beginnings of heraldry.	Identify the historical origins of a coat of arms. Interpret the elements of a coat of arms.	Restate information in own words. Design a coat of arms.
Vital Statistics	Introduce students to various vital records, such as birth, marriage and death records.	Why are these records necessary? How are these records used?	Collect data to fill in sample birth, marriage and death records. Compare collected data with an actual document.
Newspapers	Understand the basic elements of a newspaper story. Discover the five Ws and how and inverted pyramid styles of journalistic writing. Understand periodicals as primary source material.	Analyze a primary source document. Evaluate the important facts in a newspaper story.	Read for comprehension. Write an obituary using the inverted pyramid. Identify the five Ws and how in a story.
Military Service	Identify the different military records from which family information can be gleaned. Identify sources for this type of information.	Analyze primary source documents. Evaluate the importance of military service to uncovering family history.	Evaluate military records from War of 1812 and Civil War. Read for comprehension. Compare military involvement in 19th and 20th centuries.

Families

In Search of Our Past

Every family has a unique and fascinating past. The activities in this book will encourage students to investigate their families and their stories. They will learn the necessary skills that will help them seek out and discover this enthralling yet hidden past. When they have finished, they will know more about their families, and more importantly, they will know more about themselves.

Like an archaeologist, the students will have to examine many pieces of information, analyze them and fit them into the total puzzle of their family history. As they dig deeper into their families' past, they will also unearth rich knowledge about the culture, standards and ideas of days gone by.

Each section of this book deals with a different aspect of family history or with those relevant public records. Knowledge of how to use these records will help them discover and document their own personal story of how they became who they are. This book will provide them with all the necessary background knowledge, skills and tools for an intriguing and rewarding dig into their family history. How far they dig is up to them.

Families

In the space below, draw everyone whom you consider to be part of your family. Use stick figures to represent family members.

Look at your drawings. Did you include grandparents, aunts and uncles, nieces and nephews, and cousins? Did you include relatives who have died?

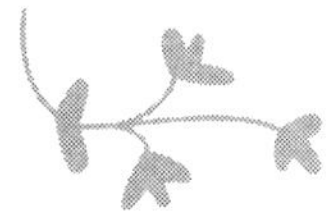 # Families 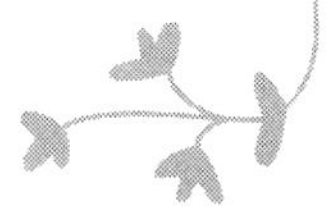

The preceding exercise helped you decide who makes up your family. Every family situation is different. Times have changed. Traditionally, a family was viewed as consisting of a father working at a job and a mother raising the children at home. This is no longer the most common family unit. Here are definitions of some family terms.

nuclear family: a family unit of parents and dependent children

extended family: a social unit of a father, mother, dependent children and other relatives (often representing several generations) living together in one household

blended family: a family unit created when two divorced or widowed parents with children marry

adoptive family: a family unit containing children legally added to household through adoption

ancestor: a person you are descended from, e.g., grandfather, great-grandmother, etc.

descendant: the offspring of an ancestor

Some family terms were used differently in diaries, letters and wills of the 1600s and 1700s. For instance, *brother* might have referred to a "brother in church," rather than a blood brother. The term *sister* was often used in the same way. Even more common and vague was the term *cousin*. This term was used when talking about nearly any relative who was not as close as son, daughter, brother or sister.

Here are some terms of social rank used in the 1600s and 1700s.

Mr.: *Mr.* was used in colonial America as a title for men of high social standing who owned land or held an important civil office.

Mrs.: *Mrs.* appears frequently in old records as an abbreviation for *Mistress*, a title given to a girl of the 1600s who came from a socially prominent family. It was also given to married women.

goodman/goodwife: These titles were given to respected men and women in the Puritan community. These titles, however, did not rate quite as high as the more respected titles, *Mr.* and *Mrs.*

deacon: In Puritan New England, *deacon* was the highest ranking title because a deacon was the highest ranking member of the church. The Puritans had a devout respect for God and for those who served God and church.

widow: A widow was (and is) a woman whose husband has died.

freeman: Many people earned their passage to America by contracting to work for a certain number of years. This practice was called indenture. People who served out the contract period, usually three to seven years, were then released from their indentures. They became free. Freemen had the same rights as other free people.

Family Relationships

Word List

affinity: relationship through marriage

blood: relationship through birth

monogamy: a marriage between one man and one woman

polygamy: a marriage practice of having two or more wives or husbands at the same time

The Family

The family has been the basic unit of every civilization since history was first recorded, and even before. The family provides a place for rearing and educating children, as well as offering emotional and social support for all its members. Although many kinds of marriages have existed throughout time and in different cultures, most societies—but not all—now recognize monogamy as the legal form of marriage.

For most modern societies, until recently, the term *family* was rigidly defined as "parents and children and all kin related by blood or affinity." (The family of birth is called the blood relationship. The family you or your blood relatives marry into is called the affinity relationship.) But today, the definition of what makes a family has been drastically altered to reflect the myriad of relationships that, although they may not fit into the traditional idea of family, are every bit as much of one.

A search for ancestry or family roots will require students to use many of the subjects they have previously studied, calling on and honing their skills in language arts, history, geography and biography. Like a detective, to uncover the clues of the past and to understand what those clues mean, the students must be tenacious, imaginative, intuitive, sympathetic, tireless, determined and reflective. In time, they will discover that cultivating these qualities will bring them rewards beyond these activities and in the years to come.

For the student following a "family trail," the search will bring fascinating insights into how chance, circumstance and love led to this exact person at this exact moment at this exact place. Most importantly, the student will begin to get an understanding of how many hundreds of people over thousands of years had to come together to ultimately create this one unique individual.

What the student discovers during these activities can offer treasure troves of genetic and environmental information, ranging from the origins of hair and eye color to the reasons a family lives where it does. History takes on a new immediacy when the forces of wars and climactic and economic changes are seen at work on the direction of one's family story. Biology comes alive when a facial feature is recognized in an aging, faded photo from a long-gone century. And the realization that one's actions can have a ripple effect for generations to come offers new understandings of how we are not only connected to those around us, but also to those who came before us and those still yet to be born. It will become clear that we live not only in a world of space, but of time as well.

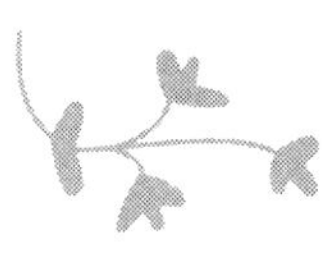 # Family Relationships 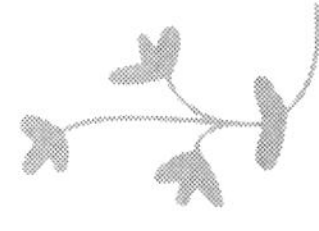

Exercise 1

Fill in the following chart with your own physical traits. After completing this part of the exercise, pause a moment to think about your parents and grandparents. From which ancestor or ancestors do you think you got each physical trait?

1. general build ____

2. eye color ____

3. complexion ____

4. hair color ____

5. hair texture ____

6. hair straightness ____

7. shape and size of hands ____

8. length and shape of feet and toes ____

Exercise 2

Begin work on your family history. Start with yourself. You have a story to tell. Answer these questions:

1. What is your full name?____

2. What are your nicknames? ____

3. What is your birth date? ____

4. Where were you born? ____

5. What time of day were you born?____

6. How much did you weigh at birth? ____

7. What was your length at birth?____

8. What is your father's full name?____

9. What is your mother's full name? ____

10. What schools have you attended? ____

Family Relationships

11. What jobs have you had? ______________________________________

12. If you are a member of a religious faith, to which one do you belong?

____

13. Where do you live? ______________________________________

14. What is your favorite food? ______________________________________

15. What pets do you have? ______________________________________

16. What are your hobbies? ______________________________________

17. What are your community activities? ______________________________________

18. What five things would you like to accomplish in your lifetime? ______________

____

19. What are your parents like? ______________________________________

____

20. What kinds of music do you like? ______________________________________

16

Pedigree

A pedigree is a written record or a chart of a line of ancestors. Look at the following two pedigree charts. One chart shows descent only along the male line–from father to son. The second chart shows descent from many different ancestral lines.

The number of ancestors from which you have directly descended doubles with every step backward into a previous generation. Thus, the ancestral pedigree chart is more difficult to complete.

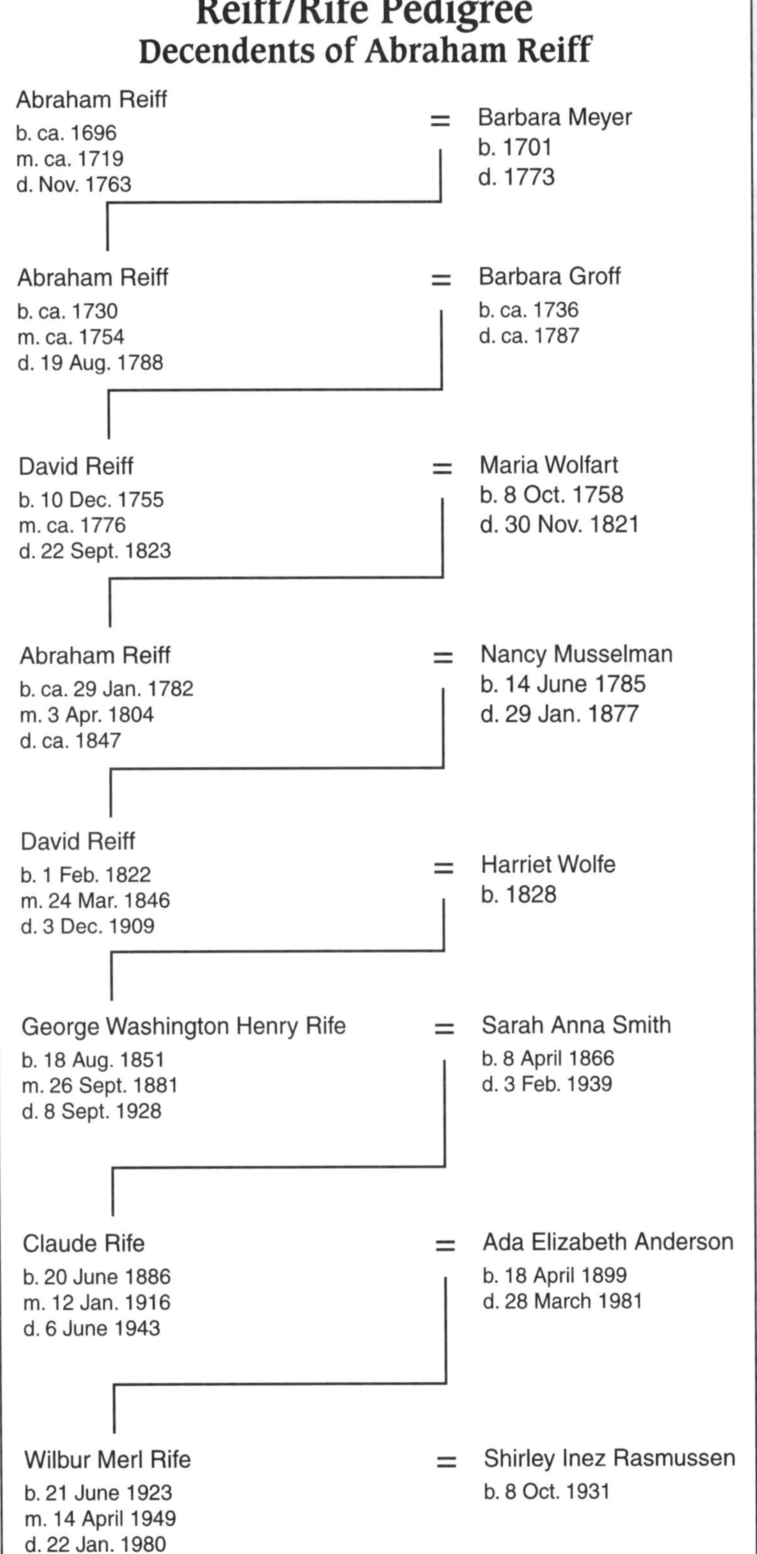

Rife Pedigree Chart

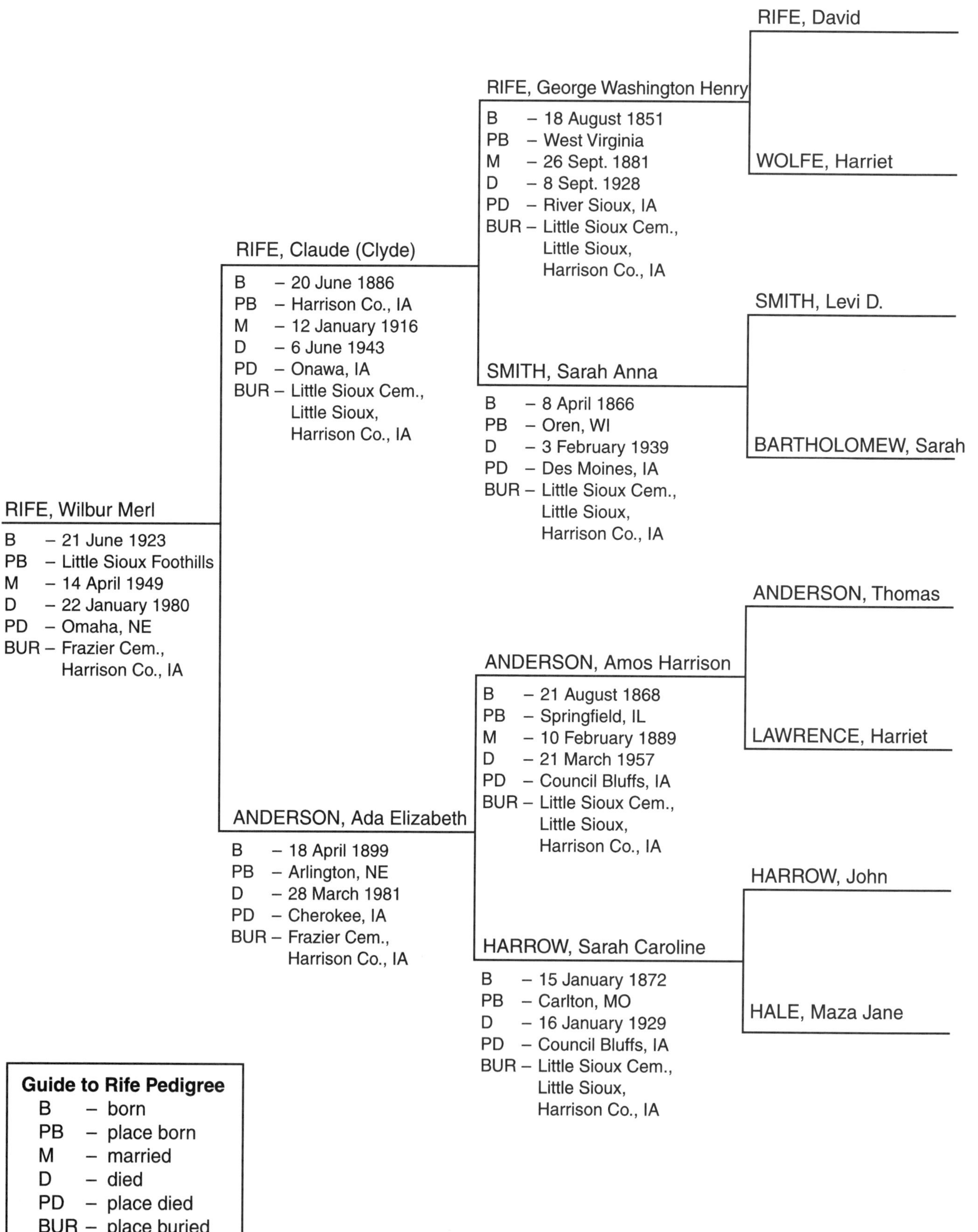

Guide to Rife Pedigree
B   – born
PB – place born
M   – married
D   – died
PD – place died
BUR – place buried

Ancestry Charts

These guidelines will help you fill out the ancestry charts.

1. Record each person's full name. Write the last name first in all capital letters, then the first name, then the middle name. (Last names are sometimes referred to as surnames.)

    Example: RIFE, George Washington Henry

2. Write the event, then the day, month and year of that event.

    Example: Died—8 September 1928

3. Always enter the smallest geographical area first. Begin with town, village or city. Then add the county and state. Add the name of the country, too, if the event occurred in a foreign nation.

    Example: River Sioux, Harrison County, IA

    NOTE: Use abbreviations for states from the post office list below.

4. Any information that you are unsure of should be followed by a question mark within parentheses.

    Example: Born—18 August 1851 (?)

5. All sources of information should be recorded.

State	Post Office	State	Post Office	State	Post Office
Alabama	AL	Louisiana	LA	Ohio	OH
Alaska	AK	Maine	ME	Oklahoma	OK
Arizona	AZ	Maryland	MD	Oregon	OR
Arkansas	AR	Massachusetts	MA	Pennsylvania	PA
California	CA	Michigan	MI	Rhode Island	RI
Colorado	CO	Minnesota	MN	South Carolina	SC
Connecticut	CT	Mississippi	MS	South Dakota	SD
Delaware	DE	Missouri	MO	Tennessee	TN
Florida	FL	Montana	MT	Texas	TX
Georgia	GA	Nebraska	NE	Utah	UT
Hawaii	HI	Nevada	NV	Vermont	VT
Idaho	ID	New Hampshire	NH	Virginia	VA
Illinois	IL	New Jersey	NJ	Washington	WA
Indiana	IN	New Mexico	NM	West Virginia	WV
Iowa	IA	New York	NY	Wisconsin	WI
Kansas	KS	North Carolina	NC	Wyoming	WY
Kentucky	KY	North Dakota	ND		

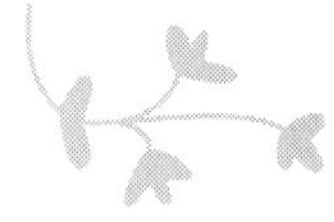 

Family Worksheet

Fill out the Family Worksheet below. Begin by writing the name of your mother and father in the appropriate spaces. Then use the guidelines given on the previous page to complete the worksheet.

FATHER
- BORN ___________________________ PLACE ___________________________
- MARRIED _________________________ PLACE ___________________________
- DIED ____________________________ PLACE ___________________________
- BURIED __________________________ PLACE ___________________________

FATHER'S FATHER _______________ FATHER'S MOTHER _______________

MOTHER
- BORN ___________________________ PLACE ___________________________
- MARRIED _________________________ PLACE ___________________________
- DIED ____________________________ PLACE ___________________________
- BURIED __________________________ PLACE ___________________________

MOTHER'S FATHER _______________ MOTHER'S MOTHER _______________

	Children's full names		Day	Month	Year	Town	County	State
1.		B						
		M						
		D						
	Spouse	BUR						
2.		B						
		M						
		D						
	Spouse	BUR						
3.		B						
		M						
		D						
	Spouse	BUR						
4.		B						
		M						
		D						
	Spouse	BUR						
5.		B						
		M						
		D						
	Spouse	BUR						

SOURCES OF INFORMATION

20

 Pedigree Chart

Fill in this skeletal ancestry chart as completely as you can. This begins your journey into your own family history.

Your Name
B

Father
B
M
D
BUR

Mother
B
D
BUR

Grandfather
B
M
D
BUR

Grandmother
B
D
BUR

Grandfather
B
M
D
BUR

Grandmother
B
D
BUR

Great Grandfather
B
M
D
BUR

Great Grandmother
B
D
BUR

Great Grandfather
B
M
D
BUR

Great Grandmother
B
D
BUR

Great Grandfather
B
M
D
BUR

Great Grandmother
B
D
BUR

Great Grandfather
B
M
D
BUR

Great Grandmother
B
D
BUR

Name____

Radial Pedigree Chart

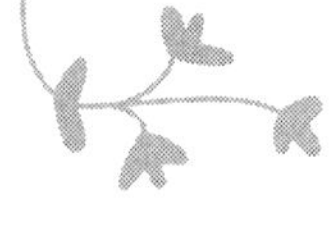

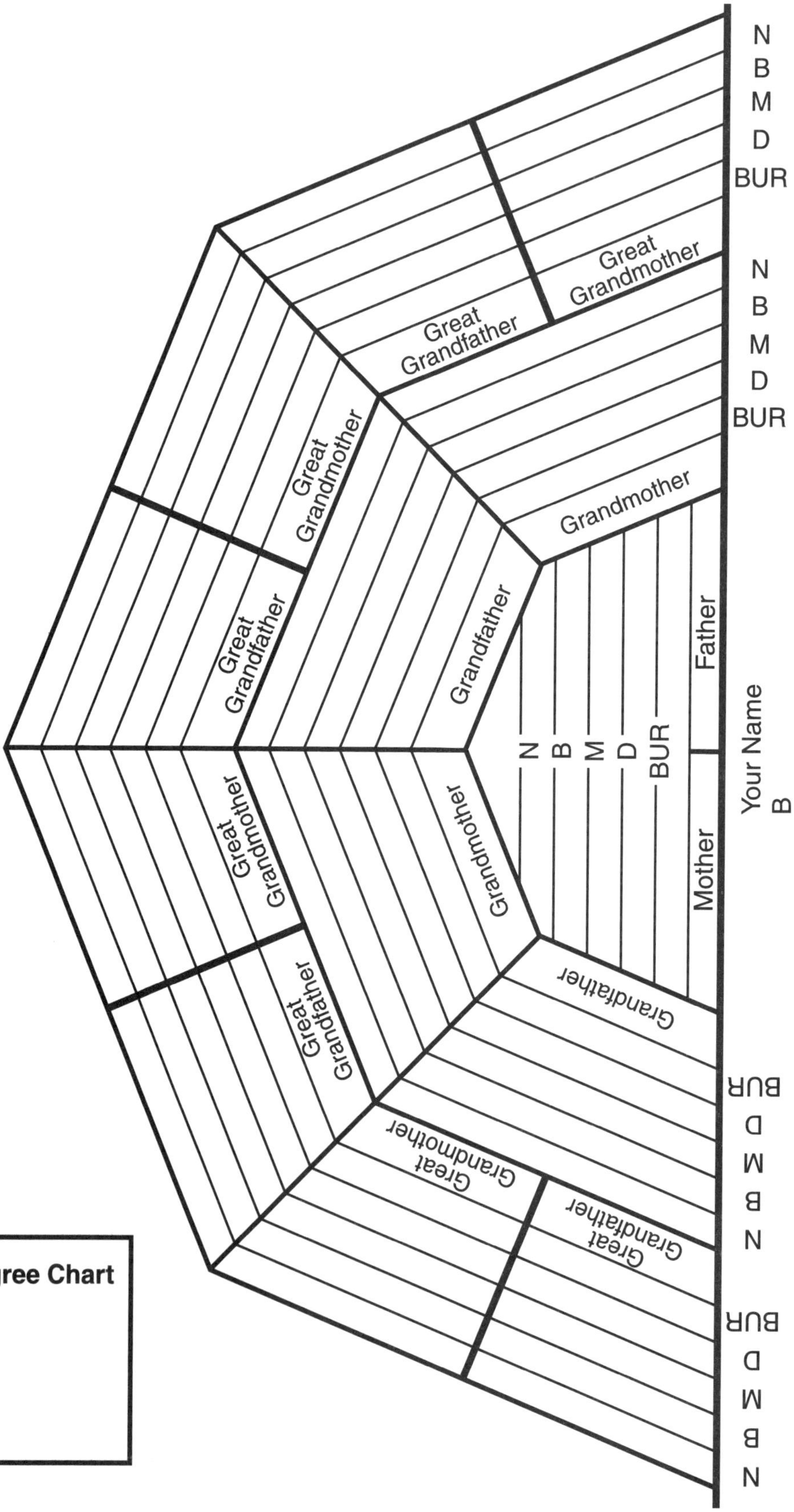

Guide to Radial Pedigree Chart

N: Name

B: Born

M: Married

D: Died

Photo Family Tree

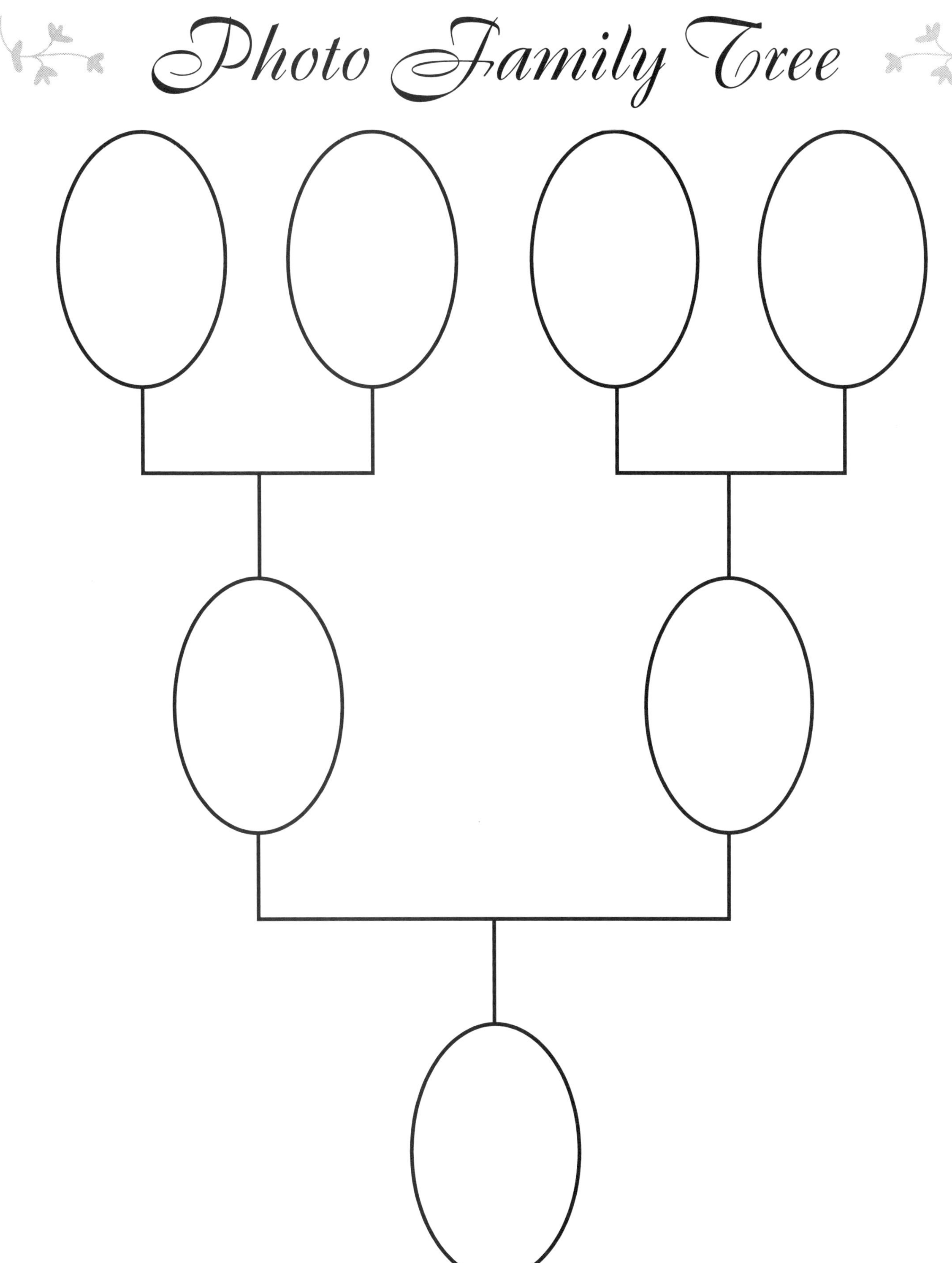

Family Records

An old family Bible can often be a rich source of family history. For many families in the past, a beautiful, leather-bound Bible was a major investment and perhaps one of the few books in the household. Because of its value and its certainty to be passed down through the generations, the family Bible was used as a repository for recording the major family milestones. Many Bibles included extra pages for just this purpose. For some pioneer families, these details, handwritten by a conscientious family member two centuries ago, may be the only source of information.

These records could include listings of births, baptisms, marriages and deaths. Often, a parent or grandparent recorded the births and baptisms of children in the family. A fortunate detective will discover children's full names, birth dates, times and places of birth, perhaps even weights and lengths listed on the Bible's endsheets. More often, however, information will be missing.

Much can be discerned from the handwriting itself. Frequently, the names and dates were painstakingly entered in elegant script, reflecting the value placed upon the family and this esteemed record of its momentous occasions. The writing could be scratchy and uncertain or strong and assured, reflecting the age or the health of the author. There could be different writing styles from recorders of different generations.

If the handwriting seems to be done in the same hand, with the same color ink, it's possible that the entries were all made at the same time, at some point after the events being recorded. This could call into question the statistics' accuracy if they were all entered from memory at a later date. (Yes, people made mistakes in the past, too.) Such information should be checked against other sources, if possible.

The family Bible was sometimes called into use as a sort of scrapbook, as well. Instruct the students to flip through the Bibles. There might well be small surprises tucked away and forgotten in the pages. Snapshots, funeral or wedding programs, clippings from local newspapers recounting noteworthy events, letters or notes written in the margins can reveal information from the past.

An old family Bible has much to tell. Even passages or parables, underlined for emphasis by some distant relative, speak to us about what the ancestor was thinking or drawing strength from during a lesson or crisis those many years ago.

Family Records

Exercise 1

If there is a Bible in your family, check to see if it has information about family members. If there is no Bible with family records in your immediate family, perhaps your grandparents or great grandparents will have one. From the Bible, copy the information about family members into a notebook. See if you can figure out how these people are related to you.

Exercise 2

If you are unable to obtain a family Bible, try other ways of getting information about your family. In your notebook, record all the births, deaths and marriages you can remember. Interview family members to get more information. Record this information for as many family members as you can. Again, don't neglect older family members as a great source of information.

Birth Announcements

Birth announcements can be a helpful source of information. These announcements usually don't contain as much information as birth certificates but are still a good fount of family history. Birth announcements are usually sent out shortly after the birth of a baby. The amount and nature of the information varies but usually contains the parents' names, the child's full name, the date of birth, and the child's weight at birth. Often, the announcement includes the baby's length at birth and sometimes the place of birth.

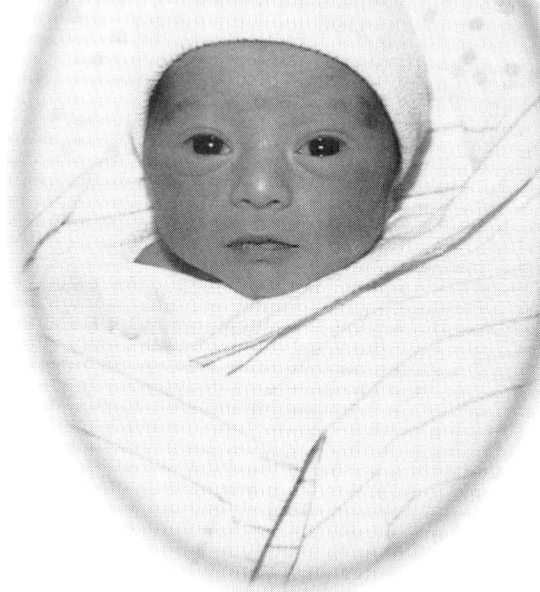

Wedding Invitations

Wedding invitations are great family documents. They are usually saved in the family Bible. A traditional wedding invitation includes the bride's name, the name of her parents, the groom's name and the name of his parents. It also includes the time, date and place the wedding is being held, along with the place the reception is being held.

Together with our parents
with joyful hearts we ask you to be present
at the ceremony uniting

Alisa Laraine Winn

and

Gibran Kahlil Hawkins

on Saturday, the twenty-second of July
Two thousand
at five-thirty in the afternoon
in the Rose Garden at the Arboretum
Arcadia, California

Funeral Programs

Funeral programs can be very helpful in researching family history. At most funerals, a program is handed out. This program usually states the name of the deceased, along with dates of birth and death. Program information also includes organizations to which the deceased belonged. Also indicated is the name of the undertaker, place and time of the funeral, place of burial and pallbearers. The program may also note the person's religious affiliation. Funeral programs are frequently found in or near where the family Bible is located.

IN MEMORY OF

WILBUR M. RIFE

DATE OF BIRTH
June 21, 1923
Mondamin, Iowa

PLACE AND TIME OF SERVICES
Schumacher Funeral Home
Logan, Iowa
Friday, January 25, 1980
11:00 a.m.

CLERGYMAN
Robert H. Evans

PLACE OF INTERMENT
Frazier Cemetery

ARRANGEMENTS BY
SCHUMACHER FUNERAL HOME
LOGAN, IOWA

MUSIC
Organ Selections
BY
Mrs. Donna Erickson

HONORARY BEARERS

C.E. Waterman   Larry Peterson

BEARERS

J.M. Hampton   John Turner
Howard Johnson   Jim Guyette
Murel Schaefer   Craig Strong

Member
Capitol Lodge No. 3, A.F. & A.M.

Masonic Service by
Chrysolite Lodge No. 420, A.F. & A.M.

Military Service by
Post No. 6256, Logan, Iowa

Local Histories

Many families have contributed their own families' story to be included in the pages of town, city and county histories. These biographies and family histories are often a wealth of information full of details about births, marriages and deaths. These histories often go beyond vital statistics to include information such as political and religious affiliations, employment history and military service. Often, these histories are more of a window into the personality of the contributor than almost any other document. By the way they are written, one can often tell what details were the most important to the writer.

Following is an example of a family history contained in the *History of Abington, Massachusetts,* published in 1866.

Stetson

The ancestor of the Stetson family, in Abington, was Robert Stetson, called Cornet Robert, because he was Cornet of the first Horse Company of Plymouth Colony, Mass. He came from England, County of Kent, and settled in Seituate in 1634. He was born 1613; died 1703. He was a prominent man in the early settlement of the Colony; was chosen a member of the Council of War in 1661, and continued in it for twenty years; in 1668, was commissioned to purchase of the Indian Sachem, Chickatabutt, a large tract of land, now comprised in the town of Hanover and Abington, for the use of the Colony, and which was subsequently re-deeded to him, together with other large grants, which shows the extent of his possessions at that time. He died at the age of 90 leaving five sons—Joseph, Benjamin, Thomas, Samuel and Robert.* Robert, the youngest, and from whom I trace my descent, resided in Pembroke.

His eldest son was named Isaac, who also lived and died in Pembroke. He had a number of sons and daughters, amongst whom was Peleg, who early removed to Abington. He raised quite a numerous family, the first of the Stetson Family in Abington of which I find any account, about 1738.

Ephraim Stetson (my grandfather), the third son of Peleg, born in 1743, located in the east part of the town, near his father; married Ruth Ford, of Abington, and pursued the cultivation of the soil for a living, and left a reputation for uprightness, honesty and piety, unsurpassed. He was deacon of the Third Congregational Church from its organization, until the infirmities of age induced him to resign the office. He lived to the great age of 96 years, in the enjoyment of almost uninterrupted good health, and with faculties unimpaired to the last,—his hopes of a happy immortality undimmed by a cloud.

His sons were Barnabas and Ephraim; his daughters were Mary, Lydia and Ruth.

Barnabas settled near his father; married Lucy Barstow, daughter of Capt. Daniel Barstow, of Hanover. His children were—Amos, Martin S., Barnabas, Lucy B., Julia A., and Lydia. His business was somewhat varied. He kept a store; manufactured shoes; also bricks; quite extensively; and carried on farming. He was associated with his brother Ephraim, in an extensive trade at Hanover Four-Corners, under the firm of B. & E. Stetson. He was an active, energetic business man through life; honest himself, he placed too much confidence, perhaps, in the honesty of his fellow-men for his own pecuniary interest. He died 1849, aged 74 years.

Martin S., now the only surviving son, commenced manufacturing boots and shoes in 1835, in company with Samuel Blake, jr., who married his sister, Julia A., and continued business in the east part of the town until the year 1842, when his business was removed to Mobile, Ala. From that time to the commencement of the war in 1861, the amount of boots and shoes (Abington's staple products) sold there annually, under the firm of M. S. Stetson & Co., will average $250,000, or, in the aggregate, $4,750,000. In June, 1857, he located with his family in South Abington. His only sone living, Amos Sumner, is the youngest and only male descendant in direct line.

The direct line of descent of this branch of the Stetson Family, is this:—

1. Robert, born 1653; 2. Isaac, born —; 3. Peleg, born 1714; 4. Ephraim, Born 1743,
5. Barnabas, born 1775; 6. Martin S., born 1809.

*This memorial was prepared by Martin S. Stetson, Esq.

Letters

Another rich source of family history can be found in letters which are often tucked away in books, or neatly tied up and carefully boxed and stored. However they are saved, letters can be a gold mine of information. Often, when families are apart, the letters family members write to each other are filled with the details of day-to-day life. These can give the reader insight to the big and small events in the letter writer's life. They can tell of triumphs and failures, happiness and joy, or of sad events and calamity—all of the drama found in each family.

The example of a letter included here is a telegram sent for Mother's Day, 1944. The telegram is written and formatted by the U.S. Army.

Family Records

Exercise 3

Write a sample birth announcement for yourself or a friend. Be sure to include as much information as you can find—time, date, birth weight, body length and place of birth.

Exercise 4

Write a sample wedding announcement for your grandparents—be sure to include as much information as possible, such as time, place, date and the bride and groom's parents' names.

Exercise 5

Write a 300-word autobiographical sketch. Base your sketch on information you supplied in previous exercises. Be sure to also include details from the Family Worksheet (page 20). Try to recall an exciting story about your family and put that into your sketch, too.

See if you can give the reader a clear picture of your life. Present details that will show that you are part of an interesting and unique family.

Exercise 6

Write a letter to your mother or grandmother. Tell her where you are and what you are doing. Write a letter as if you are in a distant place, far away from home.

Photographs

Photographs make family
history come alive. Photographs show
what ancestors actually looked like, what
they wore, even where they lived. They add color
and illumination to impersonal charts. They put faces
to names. They freeze the past forever.

Photographs also offer a peek at the culture of an era, vividly
showing how clothing styles and traditions change. Look closely at
the picture on page 33 of the two little boys, Lloyd and Evant. You
might think that the youngster wearing the dress is a girl. However, in the
1890s, when this picture was taken, boys frequently wore dresses until
about the age of three. So, obviously, clothing styles and customs do change
over the years and knowledge of this can be critical to correctly interpreting a
photo.

Look now at the wedding picture below. This couple was married in 1916. Notice
that the bride isn't wearing the traditional white. White wedding dresses came into
style later. So even traditional styles
haven't always been "traditional."
(Knowledge of these period styles can
also help date photographs when no
date is given.)

Photographs can help you keep track
of other changes, beyond clothing
styles. The photograph on page 34
captures the excitement and pride of
obtaining a new car, an early Ford,
and hints at the beginnings of
America's automotive love affair.
That is the kind of photograph that
hints at a larger history beyond
family.

Although it is certainly true that a
picture is worth a thousand
words, a photo without words
is almost valueless to the
family historian. Unknown
ancestors   become
complete strangers, with
identities   nearly
impossible to recover,
after a generation or
two has passed.
That is why
it's vital for
names

to be recorded on the backs of photos, even recently taken ones. (Make certain that the family historian identifies everyone lightly in ink on the reverse side of a photograph. Whenever possible, include time and place, too.)

When faced with a photograph with unidentified subjects, there are still a few ways to try to uncover information. The name and location of the photography studio, often appearing on family portraits, can reveal the home of the photo's subjects. That simple clue could then lead to a search of local records. A hint, a hunch and a little hard work can pay big dividends.

The most valuable method, thankfully, can also offer unexpected rewards. Show the photograph to as many relatives as possible, especially older family members. Not only might they be able to identify the subjects or recognize a location, they just might give you an added bonus of a long-forgotten memory to "flesh out" an ancestor.

The Triggered Memory
The woman had been dead for nearly 60 years when Granny was shown the photograph. By this time, Granny was nearly 90. Her face was withered. Her body was bent. As Granny stared intently at the picture, a look of recognition illuminated her face. Her pale eyes came to life. There was a rush of color to her cheeks. Then she broke into a smile, and began to tell a story about the previously unknown subject—her great Aunt Mabel, the town shrew.

*"Lord,
I remember her. She was
quite a character. She didn't like
kids, don't you know. Never had one and
never wanted one but our neighborhood was full
of 'em. Used to drive her up the wall. The worst part
was, she had an old shed, back of her house, and the
kids liked to use it for a clubhouse. No matter how many times
she chased 'em out, back they'd come.*

*"Well, one day, she gets herself a plan. She decides to rig up a bucket
of black paint over the door and the next kid that sneaks in there gets a
free coat. So she sets that bucket up but wouldn't you know it, no kids
come for a couple of days—Mabel don't know school started up— and she
forgets all about that bucket after a while."*

*Granny's eyes sparkled at the memory. "You can guess what happened. Mabel
needs something or other out of that shed and up and walks right in with nary a
thought.*

*Then Granny patted her knee and laughed to herself. "Old white-haired Mabel turned
herself into a real brunette for a couple of months. And she left those kids alone after
that, too."*

This story illustrates how an obscure photograph in the family album can make the past
richer and more immediate. Anyone's family album can do the same.

Photographs

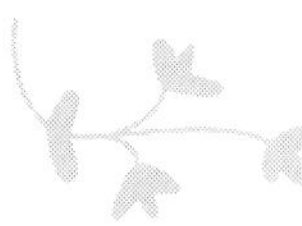

1.

2.

3.

 # *Photographs* 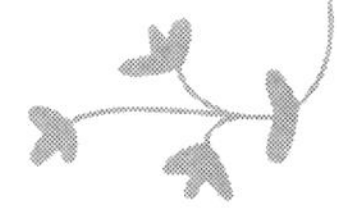

Exercise

1. Look at the picture of the couple in the first photo. Describe why you think this

   photo is special. ____

   ____

2. Study the second photo and describe the children as best as you can from what

   you see. ____

   ____

3. Look at the third photograph and describe four ways styles are different today
   for men and for women.

Men

1. ____

2. ____

3. ____

4. ____

Women

1. ____

2. ____

3. ____

4. ____

Oral History

Word List

folklore: traditions, customs, songs, stories and dances that are handed down by word of mouth from generation to generation

open question: inquiry in which the respondent is free to develop his or her own answer

closed question: inquiry in which the respondent is restricted to a narrow, specific answer

anecdote: a brief story, sometimes humorous, about an interesting personal experience

Researching family history does not always mean hours of internet or old document searches. Some of the most exciting and interesting bits of family information might not be found on a tombstone or in a dry response from a government agency.

The most fascinating treasures are to be found in the historian's own family in an interview with an older relative. Every search should include (if not begin) with family folklore—the stories that reveal and enhance the family's past.

The stories can uncover more than a lost name or forgotten relative; they could be about how grandparents met and fell in love. Or about the exploits of a notorious uncle or a famous cousin. Humorous anecdotes, high drama, exciting adventures, tragic events. These are the kinds of stories that go beyond filling out a pedigree chart. They bind a family, linking it to the past.

The more interviews that can be obtained, the better, because each individual offers his or her stories through a unique prism. Two people in a family might remember the same event differently. A grandfather may remember how tough it was to come up with the cash to pay for a short honeymoon while his wife, on the other hand, dreamily recalls the garden party that took place after the church ceremony. Different aspects hold different significance for different family members. Each version, however, only adds to the whole, makes it more three-dimensional.

Folklore
is an interpretation of an
event, rather than a cold statistic.
As a result, folklore brings color and
personality to family history, but sometimes at a
price. By its very nature, through the act of being
retold and retold, folklore changes. Each generation adds
new stories or wrinkles to old ones, embellishes, drops or
invents details. Memory is not infallible. If possible, names and
dates should be checked against more concrete sources at a later
time but never discount a story out of hand. There is truth to be found
in every tale.

Many relatives or old family friends can tell stories and relate family traditions. However, some relatives will feel more comfortable talking than others. Some will not want to talk at all. They would prefer that the past be left alone.

But, on the whole, most relatives will be eager to contribute. The best way to start an interview series is by talking to a family member with whom the family historian feels comfortable.

It's important that the interviewer knows how to ask questions that will get people to talk. That means asking questions that require more than a yes or no answer. The historian shouldn't be afraid to let the subject go off on a tangent, either. Some of the best stories are not the ones asked for but the unexpected ones, surfacing from a subconscious allowed to roam.

The best way to learn about interviewing is to study some examples. Let's take the case of Harvey Vincent. A family historian arranged to talk to Harvey. The interviewer asked Harvey questions about his father's experience in the military.

The first question invited only a one-word response. This kind of question is called a closed question. Here is an example:

Interviewer: Harvey, was your father Hiram in the Civil War?

Harvey: Yes.

This is a closed question because the person who is the subject of the interview can give only a limited and narrow response, yes or no.

Open questions have no simple answer. Open questions—sometimes called open-ended questions—set up a forum or situation for the respondent to develop an answer from his or her own experience.

Notice in the transcript on page 39 what happens when the interviewer switches to the open-ended questions. The open-ended questions set up a chance for Harvey to talk. The more open-ended questions that are asked, the more successful any interview is likely to be.

Interviewer: Harvey, was your father Hiram in the Civil War?

Harvey: Yes.

Interviewer:
What stories do you remember your father telling you about the Civil War?

Harvey: Dad was wounded in the Battle of Shiloh in April of 1862 at eight a.m. and lay on the battlefield two days and one night. He used his rifle as a crutch and hobbled under a tree. He was brought into the field hospital in a lumber wagon and the doctors sawed off his leg—no anesthetics were available at that time. The doctors and nurses thought he was dead, and they ordered him taken to the morgue. While Dad was being taken to the morgue, someone noticed him moving. He was alive. So they turned right around and took him back to the field hospital.

Hiram Vincent and his family

The
Interview Process

Francisco Lopez was born in 1918 in a small village in Mexico. Francisco and his family moved to America in 1927 and settled in Los Angeles, California.

Here is a series of questions that he might have been asked during an interview. Notice how the open questions differ from the closed questions. Open—or open-ended—questions allow the informant to add personal information and interesting details.

Open questions also make the interview more lively. Obviously, every interview will be a mix of closed and open questions, but open questions provide the most enriching information.

Closed

1. What is your last name?
2. From what country did you come to America?
3. How old were you when you came to the U.S.?
4. What is your favorite Mexican food?
5. Did you graduate from high school?
6. Where were you married?
7. Did anyone in your family serve in a war?
8. How many children do you have?
9. What is your religious preference?
10. Where are your parents buried?

Open

1. What caused your family to decide to move to America?
2. What was your home like in Mexico?
3. What do you remember most about home?
4. How was it difficult for you when you came here?
5. What were your parents like?
6. What did you enjoy most about school?
7. What kind of work did you do after graduating?
8. How did you meet your wife?
9. How did you spend your military service?
10. What event had the most profound effect on your life?

Examples of a closed and an open interview are shown beginning on page 41. Notice how the different kinds of questions prompt different responses.

Closed Interview

Interviewer: What is your last name?

Francisco: Lopez.

Interviewer: From what country did you come to America?

Francisco: Mexico.

Interviewer: How old were you when you came to the U.S.?

Francisco: Nine.

Interviewer: What is your favorite Mexican food?

Francisco: Tamales.

Interviewer: Did you graduate from high school?

Francisco: Yes. And college.

Interviewer: Where were you married?

Francisco: In Los Angeles. At St. Vibiana's.

Interviewer: Did anyone in your family serve in a war?

Francisco: Yes. I did.

Interviewer: How many children do you have?

Francisco: Five.

Interviewer: What is your religious preference?

Francisco: Catholic.

Interviewer: Where are your parents buried?

Francisco: My father is buried in East Los Angeles. My mother is buried in Mexico.

Open Interview

Interviewer: What caused your family to decide to move to America?

Francisco: We lived in a small village, near the mountains. We didn't have a lot of money, but my father grew enough food for us—corn, beans, *jitomate*—and we were happy. When I was still a little boy, fighting broke out all across the country. Government soldiers were at war with rebels and both sides were always trying to force men to join their side. My father would hide in the mountains when they would come because if they took him away, we would have no food. Once, while he was gone, my mother got very sick and died before he could return. He was different after that, changed, serious. He told me and my sister it was time to move someplace better. And so we left.

Interviewer: What was your home like in Mexico?

Francisco: Oh, it was beautiful, with mountains on one side and a stream that bubbled past us on the other. There were only perhaps 10 or 12 adobes, built next to just one dirt road. Don't misunderstand me, it was not paradise. The adobes were not grand, only one room with crumbling walls; and dusty curtains to divide the space. Thatched roofs, no windows, but it was full of pleasures for a small boy not yet old enough to work the fields.

Interviewer: What do you remember most about home?

Francisco: Although it's been many years and I was only a boy then, I still remember the smells of chiles roasting in the evening, of beans boiling, too. I remember the sound of the stream, like tiny bells. The singing of my father as he walked up the road, on his way to us after working all day. I remember the wobbly shadows on the rough walls, put there by our candle flame at night and the whispers of my mother and father across the room as I fell asleep. Those are things I will never forget.

Interviewer: How was it difficult for you when you came here?

Francisco: As difficult as it was for me, it was 10 times harder for my father. I could go to school, to catch up, but he was forced to jump right in, like a man who can't swim on a sinking boat. The truth is, I picked up English pretty quickly. Soon, I was translating newspapers and documents not only for my father but for many of our neighbors. Other than for my gringo teachers, you could imagine you were still in Mexico there were so many of us in our *barrio*. Spanish was spoken all around me.

Interviewer: What were your parents like?

Francisco: My mother, as I told you, died when I was young, so my memories are less vivid. She was small with dark, dark eyes. Very pretty with delicate features, and always smiling. Her voice was like a songbird's. My father, despite the fact that I knew him my whole life, is harder to describe. So much of him was kept inside. He never revealed his sorrows or his joys to me, at least not directly. I do remember how he pinned my first report card of all As on the kitchen wall and would study it when he thought no one was watching. So I knew he was proud of me.

Interviewer: What did you enjoy most about school?

Francisco: My teachers. Especially in elementary school. They treated me with such respect and courtesy that I felt like a person and not just a child. I wanted to do well to please them and when I answered a question correctly, their praise was like a warm ocean breeze. It was because of them that I dreamt of becoming a teacher myself.

Interviewer: What kind of work did you do after graduating?

Francisco: Well, I didn't do what I wanted to do, I'll tell you that. Everything was harder than I thought, partly because of where I came from and partly because of how little money I had. And then I fell in love and married and so earning money became more necessary than college. I did a little bit of everything, I guess—cleaning, heavy lifting, painting houses—until finally I found a position translating for an insurance office. It was dull work, but they paid me well for what I did and I probably would have stayed there for the rest of my life if not for the war.

Interviewer: How did you meet your wife?

Francisco: I wish I had some fantastic story, but the truth is Isabel sat down right next to me on the bus one day. I took one look at her and knew she was the one, but I was too shy to speak and she got off without looking at me. I rode that bus every day for two weeks just waiting for her to get on again. I almost got fired from my job. But she finally did get on again and I wasn't shy then.

Interviewer: How did you spend your military service?

Francisco: I was in the infantry, European theater. I was at Normandy and Bastogne. I won't tell you any more than that, but I will say that I saw a lot of things that made me think. And when I finally came home, I understood how short this life was. I used the GI Bill and went to college. Isabel was behind me. She must've sensed my determination. That war was awful, but it helped me become a teacher.

Interviewer: What event had the most profound effect on your life?

Francisco: That's a hard one
but if I have to make a choice, I
suppose it would be the day my first child
was born. Not only did I have all the usual
overwhelming feelings a father has then but later, when
I was holding the baby alone, I realized that she was
American, from the very first day. And I was proud and happy
for her, and for me, 'cause I'd given her a great gift. Just like my
father had done for me. I knew then, what I hadn't known before—I
love Mexico and always will . . . but America was my home.

Recording the Interview

You can trap the results of your interview in two different ways—you can take notes during the interview or you can record the interview with a tape recorder.

If you take notes, you may miss quite a bit of what is said. You will also probably miss the flavor of the interview as it comes through in the person's tone of voice. You'll find part of the fun of gathering folklore is observing how people say things.

It's also true that persons being interviewed are sometimes annoyed when an interviewer starts writing down what he or she has to say. Taking the careful notes necessary for a good interview can be a nuisance for the interviewer as well.

Some people feel equally uncomfortable around a tape recorder. For that reason, it's important to place the recorder so that it will be scarcely noticed during the interview. To keep the distraction to a minimum, be sure that your tape recorder is on and working properly before you start the interview.

Photographs and family heirlooms can be used as good prompts to touch the subject's memory or to coax out a story. The interview is a good opportunity to mine any information the subject might have about old, unidentified photographs you possess, as well.

And, finally, be sure to write the date, time and place of the interview on the tape cassette or the tape cassette case. That information will be helpful later when you produce a written transcript.

Interview Tip: If you have a camera, take a picture of the person you are interviewing.

Recording the Interview

Exercise 1

Interview someone who can provide you with information about your family. Perhaps the person is someone who is not even a member of the family. An old friend of the family sometimes can offer details that no one else knows.

For instance, if your grandfather was in World War II, an old army "buddy" might be a first-rate source of information. Check with school teachers. Often, school teachers can supply amusing anecdotes about family members who have been in their classes.

Chances are, though, you may want to begin by interviewing someone in the family. You should choose someone who knows a lot about your family history and enjoys talking about it, especially to you. You should feel comfortable around the person you interview. That is very important.

Select a familiar place for your interview, preferably a place that is friendly and relaxed. Eliminate as many distractions as you can. Turn off the radio and the television. Be considerate of the person you are going to interview. Adjust your time to fit that person's schedule.

Here are five hints to help with your interview.

1. **Be prepared.** Write out your questions in advance. Practice or go over them a few times before the interview.

2. **Use props.** Use items that will spark the memory of your informant. Photographs, newspaper clippings, old letters and family heirlooms can usually get the interview started.

3. **Be sensitive.** Do not pursue questions that make your informant uncomfortable. You do not want to cause hard feelings or alienate a valuable source of information.

4. **Be interested.** Let your informant know that you are interested. Nod your head frequently in agreement or acknowledgement that you understand. Use body language that will encourage the person to speak in a natural manner. Try to direct the conversation but, under no circumstances, attempt to control what is said. Remember, the informant's recollection is what you want to record. If you use a tape recorder, do not turn the recorder off until the informant is through speaking.

5. **Be prompt.** Be on time for the interview. Do not keep your informant waiting. The interview should last somewhere between 45e and 90 minutes. Be prompt in beginning the interview, and when the interview is over, bring it to a neat conclusion. Conclude the interview with a pleasant thank you.

Exercise 2

Write a three-page story based on the information from your interview. Unify your story with an introduction, body and conclusion.

The Internet

Nothing has changed the world of the genealogist so dramatically as the internet. Before the advent of computers, the genealogist spent much of his or her time thumbing through dusty records in courthouse basements, writing letters to churches, searching abandoned cemeteries and reading long-forgotten local histories. Now, with a modem and a mouse, much of the searching can be done from the comfort of one's own room, saving the historian hundreds, even thousands of hours of effort. The internet allows genealogists instant access to a myriad of valuable sources and sites which are growing in number every day.

Almost every topic covered in this book can be explored on the internet—church records, cemetery listings, immigration records, newspaper archives. Even if something is not directly available on the web, information to help the historian find it most likely is.

One of the most useful genealogy sites on the internet is provided by the Church of Jesus Christ of Latter-Day Saints at www.familysearch.org. The LDS Church has a larger collection of family history data than anyone else on Earth. This collection is growing constantly as more and more information is systematically indexed and posted on the internet.

Individual families have also placed their own pedigrees on the site, which are searchable. When looking for a certain deceased ancestor, type the first and last names in the appropriate boxes and click SEARCH. The more information filled on the screen, the narrower and more focused the search becomes, eliminating responses of people with the same name but with different spouses, different parents, different locations or different time periods. These searches are free.

There are other sites, such as ancestry.com, that offer searches of other data banks, such as censuses, military records or other available and indexed vital statistics, for a fee.

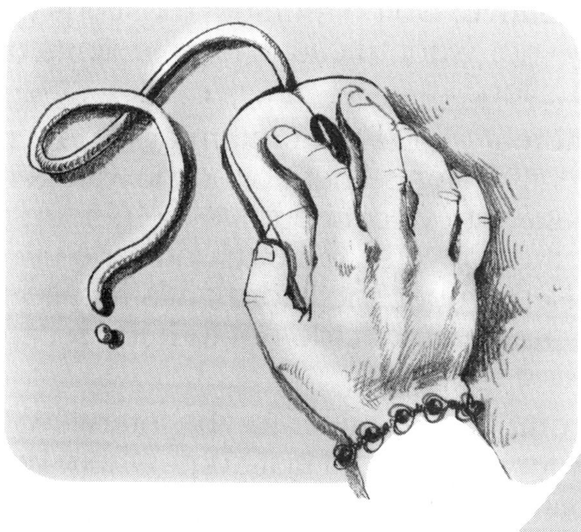

Once all of the family resources have been explored for as much information as possible, the internet should be the very next place to start. It is, undoubtedly, the genealogist's most powerful tool.

Religious Records

Churches and synagogues
have been keeping track of their
members for hundreds of years, often long
before governments began recording vital family
information. For Judaism and Christianity, tracing lines
of genealogy played important roles from their very
beginnings, reflecting the importance of ancestry and
bloodlines in religious belief. But as time passed and priorities
shifted, the following of family lines became mainly the concern of
nobility. It took the Reformation and the consequent loss of power,
territory and membership in the Roman Catholic Church to revitalize
religious record keeping in Christianity. As more Northern European countries
embraced Martin Luther's call for change in 1517 and moved to Protestantism,
the Catholic Church felt compelled to close ranks and enumerate its members.

Roots of Church Record Keeping

In 1547, at the Council of Trent, the Roman Catholic Church decreed that records of birth, marriage and death should be kept. Many of the new Protestant churches followed suit in this battle for souls.

However, wars, fires, political shifts and population migrations have had devastating effects on what information is available from this period until very recently. For instance, during World War II, invading soldiers and refugees in Europe burned tons of church records and papers to keep warm.

During the 16th and 17th centuries, many European countries established new state churches. While Southern Europe and France remained solidly Catholic, Scandinavian countries followed the Lutheran Church. The Anglican Church eventually held sway in England. In Scotland, it was the Presbyterian Church. And most of Eastern Europe followed the Eastern Orthodox Church.

Some colonies in America continued the pattern. The Episcopalian Church (Anglican) became the established church in Virginia and the Congregational Church dominated New England. As new sects and religions increasingly sought havens in America, they often discovered the same religious persecution they had fled. This forced them to move to new, little-populated areas to find the freedom of worship they sought—for example, the Baptists to Rhode Island, the Quakers to Pennsylvania and the Lutherans to the Midwest. Consequently, knowledge of an ancestor's home region in early America can offer clues to his or her religious affiliation and, possibly, to the country of origin.

This rapidly began to change, however, in 1788, with the passage of the First Amendment of the Constitution, which guaranteed religious freedom in the U.S. and set the blurring of the religious territorial boundaries in motion.

The
type of records kept by
churches hasn't changed much in
the nearly 500 years since the Council of
Trent. Churches and temples still keep
information on baptisms or births, marriages and
burials or deaths of their members. Unfortunately, the
accuracy and completeness of these records can vary widely
between denominations, parishes or places of worship,
depending on the skills of the record keepers or clerks. In an effort to
keep what remains intact, many denominations have transferred their
individual church records to national archives.

Here is a list of some of the church archives in the United States:

American Baptist Historical Society
110 South Goodman Street
Rochester, New York 14620

American Catholic Historical Association
Catholic University of America
Washington, D.C. 20017

**Church of Jesus Christ of
Latter-Day Saints**
Genealogical Department
50 East North Temple Street
Salt Lake City, Utah 84150

**Congregational Christian
Historical Society**
14 Beacon Street
Boston, Massachusetts 02108

Archives of Greek Orthodox Archdiocese of North America
10 East 79th Street
New York, New York 10021

Friends Historical Library
Swarthmore College
Swarthmore, Pennsylvania 19081

Lutheran Ministerium of Pennsylvania Historical Society
Lutheran Theological Seminary
7333 Germantown Avenue
Philadelphia, Pennsylvania 19119

**Mennonite
Historical Society**
Bluffton College
Bluffton, Ohio 45817

Moravian Archives
North Main at Elizabeth
Bethlehem, Pennsylvania 18015

Archives of Mother Church
First Church of Christ Scientist
107 Falmouth Street
Boston, Massachusetts 02110

Presbyterian and Reformed Church Historical Foundation
Assembly Drive
Montreat, North Carolina 28757

**Protestant Episcopal Church
Historical Society**
606 Rathervue Place
Austin, Texas 78700

Family information, including vital statistics as well as membership records and meeting minutes, from many Jewish synagogues has been donated and collected by archivists, as well. Here are two sources to explore:

American Jewish Archives
3101 Clifton Ave.
Cincinnati, Ohio 45220

American Jewish Historical Society
2 Thornton Road
Waltham, Massachusetts 02154

Religious Records

Exercise 1

Write the letter of the church most closely connected with the geographical area.
Some letters will be used more than once.

______	1. Virginia	a.	Catholic
______	2. New England	b.	Protestant Episcopalian
______	3. Scandinavian countries	c.	Presbyterian
______	4. Scotland	d.	Lutheran
______	5. France	e.	Congregational
______	6. Southern Europe	f.	Eastern Orthodox
______	7. Eastern Europe		

Exercise 2

In the space provided, write a short answer to each of the following questions.

1. What is an "established" church? ___________________________________

   ____

2. What was the Roman Catholic conference called that decreed the keeping of

   records? ____

3. What kinds of records can be found in a church or synagogue? ___________

   ____

4. Which constitutional amendment guarantees freedom of religion in America?

   ____

Diaries & Journals

Students are lucky indeed if
their families have any diaries that
may have been kept by family members.
Journals and diaries provide much more than
names and dates; they can provide records of the
events, both mundane and powerful, as well as the
emotions and thoughts, of our ancestor's day-to-day lives.

An ancestor's dreams, hopes, failures, longings and fears are often
revealed in a journal or diary. The family historian who looks closely
can find in these priceless records a rich legacy of how people lived.

By studying a diary, the historian can discern many facts about family
members and their friends, uncover clues about their culture and concerns,
and gain insights into an ancestor's character and life. In essence, a diary is a
window into a long-gone world.

Have the students read excerpts from the Charles Staley diary
beginning on page 52.

The
information found in
diaries will usually answer these
kinds of questions about ancestors:

What did they do for fun? What kind of work did they do? What was important to them? Where did they live? Who were their friends? What memorable things happened? What were some of their successes? How were their days spent? What did they eat? Where did they travel?

The following diary entries were written in 1870 by a young man named Charles Monroe Staley. Charles worked on a local paper in Greenfield, Adair County, Iowa.

Charles played guitar and banjo in a local band. This band was known as the Black Bird Troupe, which he abbreviates B.B. Troupe.

Charles' diary mentions several of his friends. The two friends most frequently mentioned are "Ham" and Annie. No one is sure who Ham was or what happened to him, but three years later, Charles and Annie were married.

In general, the original spelling and punctuation have been retained in order to maintain the flavor of Mr. Staley's experience. Any flaws in expression are themselves significant in reaching an understanding of this 19th century American.

January, Sunday 2. 1870
Went to church twice, very pleasant sunshine.

January, Monday 10. 1870
Very pleasant day. Ditto with Sunday morning except signing pledge, went to machine shop with Annie and the rest before dinner. Had a good appetite, practiced music and rehearsed in the afternoon. A larger audience in attendance than on Saturday night. Had a dance after performance and after dance all was lovely and the goose hung high, went to bed at 3 a.m. A jolly boy all the way from Fontanelle with the rest of Sandy's brothers, Charlie and I slept together and well Jim and Amos.

January, Friday 14. 1870
Run of the rest of the papers, put up mail. Rilburn came back, bought tambourine cost $2.50. Troupe met and practiced music in the auditors office in the courthouse.

January, Monday 17. 1870
Very cold, 7-9 degrees below zero. Windy all day—done Rilburns chores and boarded there. Was in the office all day. B.B. Troupe met in auditors room in courthouse in evening and practiced–not very well. Busted my tambourine.

January,
Sunday 30. 1870

Well in the office all day, went to saloon and got oysters for dinner. Wrote a letter to M.N. There seems to be a disappointment among the women in regard to my going with some ladies a riding. I was more interested in some other business that was more to my benefit consequently, I did not go. Pretty rough day.

Cash Account—January

Date		Received	Paid
1	New Years Gift	2.00	
1	Sunderies		1.50
8	" "		.25
14	Tambourine		2.50
18	Peruvian Bitters		1.00
19	Medicine		.45
21	Cove Oysters		.60
24	Medicine		.30
25	Cove Oysters		.65
"	Postage Stamps		.15
1	Cash on Hand	22.00	
28	Oysters and Candy		.40
"	Cloth for Coat—B.B.		.55
	Amt. Paid out		8.35
31	Balance in Hand	13.65	

February, Tuesday 1. 1870

In the office all day set type nice day very windy, got a letter from Sallie Ridenour, B.B. Troupe met in evening and practiced in Saloon for a while, and then went to our office.

February, Thursday 3. 1870

A nice day, worked pretty hard all day setting type. Ham not very well, Got a new tambourine head by mail, went to bed at 11.

February, Monday 21. 1870

Nice day, set type, the opinion of the majority of persons that were to our performance is that it was well worth a quarter, retired at 10.

Cash
Account—February

Date		Received	Paid
1	Amt. in hand	13.65	
2	To Candy		.10
6	To Sundries		.15
10	To B.B. Shirt		1.40
11	To Dramatic Show		.25
"	To Greenfield Exp.		1.10
12	To More Cloth for B.B.C.		.20
26	To Sundries		.10
	Amt. Paid out		3.30
28	Balance in Hand	10.35	

March, Tuesday 15. 1870

Snow storm still raging impossible to be out doors. Did not go to dinner. Ham & I had balounie sausage and crackers for our grub, retired early snow storm still in all its fury to bad for B.B. Troupe to practice.

March, Sunday 20. 1870

Was in the office all day, wrote a letter Sallie Ridenhour and read most of the day retired early, Ella Hetterington and Wesley Rodgers were married in the evening at 8 o'clock but few that knew it.

March, Monday 21. 1870

Nice day, considerable excitement about the wedding. 'Do not feel very well'. The youthful deportment of Fontanelle formed a chivalree company "musical instruments consisting of tin pans. Cow bells, tin cans, fire arms" for the married couple, but the music being so discordant was concluded to treat.

March, Tuesday 22. 1870

Nothing of any importance occurred today, tolerable nice day, The BB Troupe met and was to meet and practice in the evening, some of the boys got stubborn because they did not all meet when they were ready, so they would not meet to practice at all met at the office and held sort of a Quaker meeting but prospects were better for the troupe to break up than anything else.

March, Wednesday 23. 1870

Opinion of the BB troupe that it is Busted, Gloomy day. do not feel well, set type all day retired early.

March, Saturday 26. 1870

Nice day. Set type in the forenoon, had lots of fun in afternoon Annie H. Gertie C. and Feriss Shreves were in to see Ham & me—took my ring. did not work in the evening was to Dan Marquets awhile and then to Uncle Tom's Cabin for first time, The scene there

would
have been interesting for
an artist to draw, took a few notes
as warning and then retired 11 o'clock.

March, Thursday 31. 1870

Finished running of papers and put up for mail, weather
still gloomy trying to rain, roads bad — I am getting better
feel like work, went to bed at 10 o'clock. Anna H. brought her
dollar club tickets, _____(blank)______ Ham was to dinner.

April, Tuesday 5. 1870

Pleasant weather, worked in the office all day, nothing new. No news by
mail but Columbus Gazette retired at 10 o'clock BB Troupe practiced at Court
House in evening. J. Hetherington "Bones player" was with us, Club concluded
to take him in the club.

April, Friday 15. 1870

Tolerable nice day but pretty cold, worked all day went to a surprise party in the
evening at Wesly Rodgers. The girls arranged it and took the boys there. Annie was
my pardner had a gay time played a while and then danced and went home as happy
as we come retired about 12-1/2 all right but sleepy.

April, Saturday 16. 1870

Cold and snowed. Done some colored work. "Posters for Rilburn & Ruth" Set type in the
afternoon. Ham and I had a long dispute both mad for awhile. Got a letter from Thee time
of writing this F. Fuller is sawing away on his old fiddle and Mr. R. is working his feet,
Ham is playing his Harmonica 1/2 past 8 and in the office all right. Don W. was to town
today.

April, Monday 18. 1870

Pleasant day, set type all day, nothing of excitement occurred today. Ham and I had
some music this evening I feel all right now days. My eyes frequently would take an
involuntary glimpse out of the window to spy a fair maid then would go skipping
around the house across the street exercising herself on domestic duties. "What might
her name be"—

April, Wednesday 20. 1870

Set type in forenoon prepared wrappers after dinner while Ham got the forms
ready to run off the papers in the morning went serenading in the evening,
with all the Black Birds except Bones Practiced a while at Charlie's first went
to the Pacific House played a while–were all requested to come to Uncle
Tom's Cabin–Then went to Bailey's and from there to Jim Taylors. More
"O be joyful" Some girls came danced one set took my Prairie flower
home, retired for the night.

April, Thursday 21. 1870

Nice day. Run off the papers by noon done up for mail
in the afternoon, was a nice warm day, went to a
party at J. Taylors in the evening took Anna
party over by ten o clock took my fair
damsal home and retired.
Played guitar.

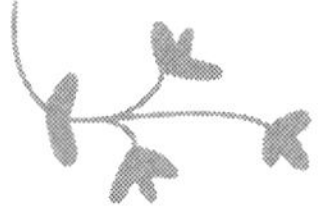

Diaries & Journals

Exercise 1

Here are some of the terms found in Mr. Staley's journal. See if you can figure out what each word means from the way he uses it in the sentence. Correct the spellings as necessary.

goose hung high _______________________________

jolly boy _______________________________

chivalree _______________________________

bones player _______________________________

gay time _______________________________

serenading _______________________________

What terms or expressions do you use today that might sound strange to someone a century from now? List three of these phrases or slang words and their meanings.

1. _______________________________

____

2. _______________________________

____

3. _______________________________

____

Exercise 2

Keep your own journal for seven days. Your journal will become a written record of your life for one week. Observe closely the world around you. Write your observations and feelings in your journal.

Day 1

Charles frequently says that it was a "nice day." That alone does not really describe the weather. What was the temperature'? Was the sun shining or did it rain? Were the birds singing? Was the grass green? Were the flowers blooming? On the first day of your journal, describe the weather. Be specific. If it is a nice day, explain why. Specific details will help people understand what you consider a nice day.

Journal – Day 2

Day 2

Through Charles' diary, we know that he liked oysters. At least he ate them several times. He also ate a meal of "balounie sausage and crackers." From this information, we get an idea of the food that may have been popular in 1870.

On Day 2, write down everything that you eat and drink, including snacks. Keep an exact record from the time you get up in the morning until you go to bed at night. If you eat in a restaurant or pick something up at the grocery store, write down the price of the meal or item. Records like these help historians reconstruct the lives of people who lived during an earlier time.

Day 3

On the entry for March 26, 1870, Charles writes *took my ring*. This vague passage refers to his engagement to Annie, whom Charles later married. Because Charles did not elaborate, we don't know how he felt about the event. We can imagine that he was happy, although he does not say so.

On your third day, write about something that happens. The event you write about doesn't have to be as important as an engagement. It could be something as simple as going to the store.

After you record the event, explain your feelings about it. Had you wanted to go? Were you disappointed in how high the prices were? Were you angry that you didn't have more money? Or were you happy because you saw someone you knew? Describe what happened and explain your feelings.

Journal – Day 4

Day 4

Charles lives in Iowa but takes the *Columbus (Ohio) Gazette.* Charles may be interested in a newspaper from another state because it's where his brother lives or because Charles himself had once gone to school there. At any rate, we know that Charles reads an out-of-state newspaper. List the different things you read in a day. Why do you read them? Are you studying for school or just glancing at a newspaper? Do you like the newspaper? What publications do you or your family subscribe to? Why?

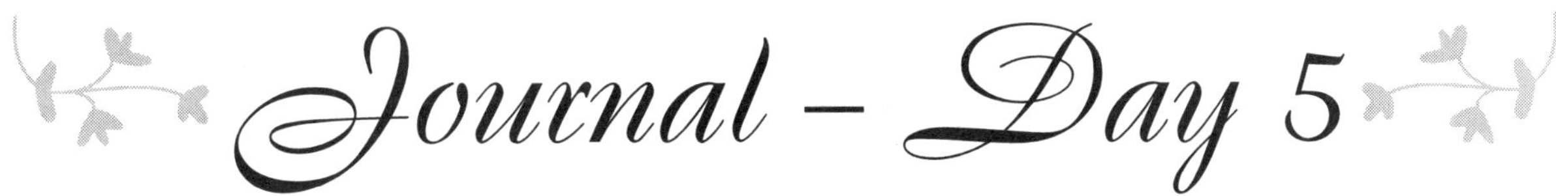

Journal – Day 5

Day 5

Charles Staley works for a local paper. He sets type, helps with the printing, wraps the papers and gets them ready to mail. We know that Charles did this because he makes brief statements in his journal about his day at the newspaper office.

In your journal, tell about your work. If you don't have a job, describe the job of a friend or relative. What is the job? What is a workday like? How long are the hours? How hard is the work? What does it involve? Are there special machines to operate? What are your feelings about the job?

Journal – Day 6

Day 6

Music takes up much of Charles' spare time. He plays a banjo and guitar in the Black Bird Troupe. He also likes to dance.

List the recreational activities that you enjoy. Is your favorite recreational activity watching television? What are your favorite programs? How long do you watch? Do you have cable TV? Is your television a color set? Do you watch with your family or friends?

Describe what you did for fun today, whether it was reading at the library or swimming in the local pool. Then give a detailed account of whom you were with, where you were, how much whatever you did cost and how long the activity took.

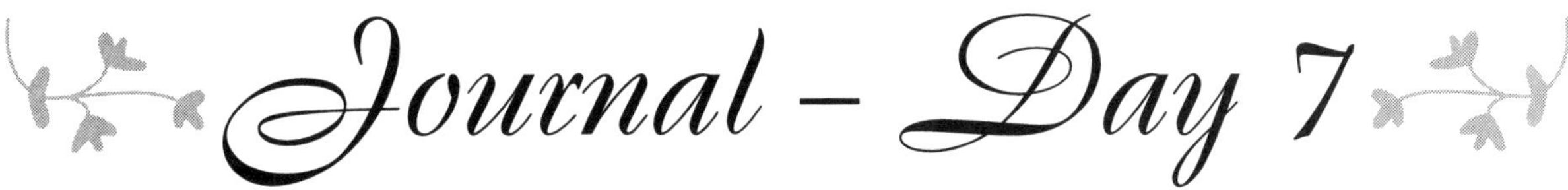

Journal – Day 7

Day 7

Write down what happened today. Record anything and everything you do and the people you are with. Record all of the sights, smells, textures and sounds. Record your feelings. Are you happy or sad? Why do you feel the way you do?

 # Cash Account 

Exercise 3

List all of your expenses for one month. Select an item Charles Staley purchased in 1870, and do price comparisons with the same items today. What conclusions can you draw?

Cemeteries

Burying the dead is the earliest known human ritual. Perhaps as long as 75,000 years ago, Neanderthals began to inter the remains of their deceased loved ones. Probably not long after that, humans felt compelled to mark the site to let others know someone of importance had passed on.

We continue this tradition today, announcing to the world the vital statistics of our existence by carving our names, dates of birth and death and perhaps an epitaph on our gravestones.

But names and dates are not the only pieces of information to be uncovered in a cemetery. There is another language, a secret language of art and symbolism, waiting to be discerned from the stones and statuary. Even the shapes and sizes of the tombstones have much to tell us about the dead's gender, age and, of course, wealth.

Symbolism

A couple took along their six-year old son to visit the gravesite of his grandfather. After they had placed flowers on the grave, the boy wandered off to study the cemetery, fascinated by all the different shapes and carvings on the gravestones.

His parents noticed that he was particularly taken with a few smaller gravestones. When he returned with his parents to the car, he sat silently for a moment, mulling over what he had seen. Finally, he spoke: "Why did so many people want to be buried next to their sheep?"

The boy had noticed carvings of lambs on several smaller stones and assumed animals were buried there. Unknown to the boy, however, the lambs were actually symbols of innocence, often carved on the gravestones of young children.

This story illustrates how a common graveyard symbol–the lamb–can be misinterpreted. To get the full significance of the cemetery environment, you should have a general familiarity with the symbols you find. The family historian who understands this symbolism can read the silent messages of the cemetery, can hear the quiet whisperings of the dead.

Burial scene, Grand Island, Nebraska, 1912

Here are some of the more
common symbols and their meanings.

angel: A recurring symbol of Christianity, the angel represents God's messenger. It also symbolizes resurrection, nativity, and the annunciation (the announcement to Mary that she would bear Jesus). The angel with one hand extended symbolizes guardianship.

clasped hands: Clasped hands symbolize holy matrimony. Cuffs and ribbed sleeves are often shown, too. The woman's hand is on the left, and the man's hand is on the right. The man's forefinger is often extended and pointing downward.

clover: Clover represents the Trinity, i.e., the Father, the Son and the Holy Ghost. It also represents St. Patrick.

cross: The cross is universally recognized as the symbol of Christianity. The cross appears in many different forms. It is frequently used in connection with other symbols. The anchor cross represents hope in Christ (Hebrews 6:19). The cross and the crown are symbols of the passion and crucifixion of Christ. The Latin cross symbolizes redemption, faith and atonement.

crown: The crown represents rank, sovereignty, royalty, eternal life, reward and honor and the Lord's kingly office.

dove: The dove represents the Holy Spirit as seen in Mark 1:10 of the Bible. It also symbolizes peace, purity, meekness and humility.

gate to heaven: The gate to heaven represents the Virgin Mary.

grapes and grape leaves:
Grapes and grape leaves symbolize
the Eucharist, the blood of Christ. Clusters of
grapes on a vine represent the Lord and followers,
the Church and unity.

ivy: Ivy symbolizes memory, fidelity
and immortality.

lamb: The lamb represents the Lord as
the Good Shepherd. It also represents
innocence.

lily: The lily symbolizes purity, innocence,
heavenly bliss, majestic beauty, marriage and
Christ's resurrection.

lily of the valley: The lily of the valley is
symbolic of humility and purity.

mansions in the sky: The symbol of a mansion
or castle-like buildings and clouds is from John
14:2: "In my Father's House are many mansions;
if it were not so, I would have told you. I go to
prepare a place for you."

oak leaves and acorns: Oak leaves and acorns symbolize courage, strength, eternity, force and virtue.

open book: An open book symbolizes the Bible, the Word of God, the divine authorship.

pointing fingers: Pointing fingers represent the hand of God and benediction.

rose: The rose has two sets of meanings, religious and the worldly. Religiously, it symbolizes the Lord, Messianic hope and the Nativity. The roses on a cross symbolize the death of Christ. The rose also represents love and two of its own qualities, beauty and perfection.

sunburst: A sunburst symbolizes the dawn of life.

three leaves and a hanging bud: The meaning of this symbol can be seen in the following two epitaphs for a child:

As the angels were passing

They saw a flower and picked it.

Budded on Earth

To bloom in Heaven.

Both epitaphs make a comparison between the child's life and a flower. The second epitaph indicates the child died too young to have "bloomed" or reached maturity on Earth; therefore, the child will do so in Heaven. A broken bud represents death at a young age, and the three leaves represent the Trinity.

wheat: Wheat is symbolic of the Eucharist, the body of Christ.

willow: The willow symbolizes sorrow and grief. The following epitaph conveys that meaning:

There's a fresh little mound 'neath the willow,

Where at evening I wander and weep.

There's a dear vacant spot on my pillow,

Where a little face used to sleep.

winged death's head: The winged skull represents death and the soul flying away from this Earth. A once common motif on early New England tombstones, it has since evolved into a winged cherub.

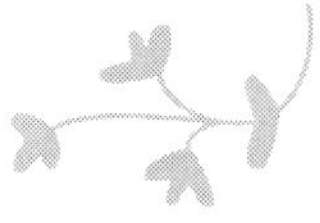

Gravestone Rubbing

Exercise 1

Cemeteries are filled with gravestones that have beautiful script and symbolism.

Make a rubbing of a family member's gravestone or of a gravestone you think is beautiful. Pick a stone that has a smooth, clean surface.

But be careful. Do not choose a fragile stone. Pressure may cause it to chip, crack or break. Pressure can also cause the face of a fragile stone to flake and separate.

Old gravestones are an important part of our heritage. They are folk art treasures that should be treated with care and respect.

Some cemeteries do not allow people to make gravestone rubbings. Research and respect the rules of the cemeteries where you plan to make your rubbings.

How to Make a Gravestone Rubbing

Materials

masking tape
scissors
paper
bottle of water
soft bristled brush
rubbing wax or chalk

Procedure

Step 1
Choose a solid gravestone, one that is not fragile or crumbling. Make sure letters, numbers, symbols and any ornamentation are clearly etched. Clear etching is more important than deep etching. Deeply etched carvings or high relief carvings may cause the paper to tear.

Step 2
Clean the face of the gravestone with water and a soft bristled brush. It's important to wash away all bird droppings, leaves and as much grime as possible.

Step 3
Cut the paper you will be using to a size larger than the face of the gravestone. Place the paper over the entire stone, so the stone will be protected from damage while you work. Tape the paper on all four sides. The paper must be solidly in place and remain that way while you do your rubbing.

Step 4
Begin your rubbing by stroking lightly across the paper. Stroke with the flat broad part of your chalk or wax. Soon your design will begin to appear. Continue stroking until the image area builds to the darkness you want.

Step 5
Remove your rubbing. Write the name of the deceased, the date of death, the name of the cemetery and location and the date you made the rubbing. Chalk rubbings should be sprayed with a fixative to keep them from smearing.

Some Tips on Choosing Paper: To start, you may just want to use average weight wrapping paper. Wrapping paper is inexpensive and works just as well as papers that cost a lot more. As you get better, you can switch to a rice paper or vellum tissue if you want your rubbing to take on the look of a work of art.

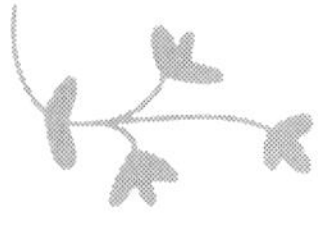 # Cemetery Symbolism 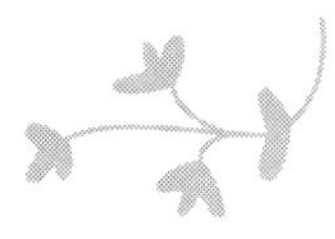

Exercise 2

1. How would you define *symbolism*? Consult a dictionary if you need help.

____

____

2. Why are cemeteries important to family historians?_______________

____

____

3. What kinds of information can you find on gravestones? _______________

____

____

Exercise 3

Write the letter of the meaning most closely associated with the symbol.

______ 1. dove   a. dawn of life

______ 2. lamb   b. Christ's resurrection

______ 3. angel   c. the Good Shepherd, innocence

______ 4. crown   d. sovereignty, royalty, Lord's kingly office

______ 5. ivy   e. peace, purity, meekness and humility

______ 6. lily   f. memory, fidelity and immortality

______ 7. rose   g. love, beauty, perfection

______ 8. sunburst   h. God's messenger to man

Epitaphs

Remember me as you pass by,
As you are now, so once was I.
As I am now, so must you be,
Prepare for death and follow me.

An epitaph is an inscription on a gravestone or tomb marking the memory of a dead person. The epitaph you have just read can be traced back to 14th century England. Its message reminds passers-by of their own mortality.

Epitaphs are a dying literary form. Seldom used on modern gravemarkers, epitaphs are to be found almost exclusively on older gravestones. Today, as a result of age and weathering, these epitaphs are rapidly disappearing from the cemetery scene. But there are still many old graveyards rich with epitaphic art and poetry.

Many epitaphs were selected by people before they died, often from epitaph books. Of course, not all epitaphs originated this way. Some were written by family members or close friends. Some of the more tender epitaphs that mark the gravestones of children were probably written or selected by grieving parents. Some people preferred to write their own epitaphs while living. Thomas Jefferson wrote his own. His epitaph includes what Jefferson thought to be the major accomplishments of his life.

Here was buried Thomas Jefferson.
Author of the Declaration of American Independence and of the statute of
Virginia for religious freedom and
father of the University of Virginia.

(Notice he didn't mention being third President of the U.S.)

Some epitaphs were written as a curse to keep people from disturbing the remains of the dead. William Shakespeare's epitaph is a verse written to discourage just such activity. Incidentally, Shakespeare's grave has been left undisturbed for almost 400 years.

Good friend for Jesus' sake forbear,
To dig the dust enclosed here;
Blessed be the man that spares these stones,
And cursed be he that moves my bones.

As noted, some of the more poignant verses may be found on children's gravestones. The following epitaph appears on the gravestone of a five-day-old infant who died in 1874.

My beauteous child with lids of snow,
Closed are thy dim blue eyes.
It cheers a mother's heart to know,
They shine beyond the skies.

Other epitaphs are messages
from the deceased, expressing a belief
in the afterlife.

Beneath this stone I've placed in trust
Not the immortal, but the dust
Of one on Earth to one most dear
Who learned in youth their God to fear.
God in His wisdom has recalled
The boon His love had given
And though the body moulders here
The soul is safe in Heaven.

The Bible is also a much-used source of epitaphs. Many gravestones have Bible verses carved upon them.

Blessed are the dead which die in the Lord. (Revelations 14:13)

Blessed are the pure in heart for they shall see God. (Matthew 5:18)

Epitaphs can be as short as one word: *Gone.* Or they can be several stanzas long. Some are sad. Others are amusing: *I told you I was sick.* Sometimes they are meant to honor the deceased. Sometimes they are meant to comfort the survivors. But all of them supply valuable insights for the family historian.

Military Graves

Men and women who have died for their country have a special place in the hearts of Americans. Entire cemeteries have been set aside exclusively for the burial of those who have served in the armed forces. The National Cemetery at Arlington, Virginia, where thousands of veterans from nearly every war are buried, is an example.

The gravestones of service men and women buried in national cemeteries are usually marked with great simplicity and dignity. The name of the service person and his or her record of service are about the only pieces of information offered on most military graves. However, on earlier military graves, epitaphs were commonplace. Here is an epitaph found on a Union Civil War veteran's grave.

Sweet be thy rest O soldier brave
Let angels guard thy hallowed grave
And while the stars in Heaven flame
Let glory wreath thy honored name.

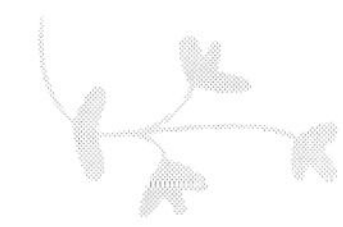
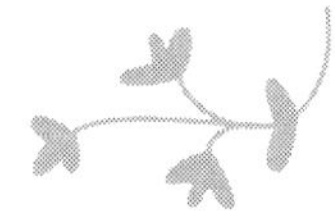

Epitaphs

Exercise 4

1. What are epitaphs? ____

2. Who writes epitaphs? ____

3. Name two sources for epitaphs. ____

Exercise 5

Go to a cemetery and record 10 different epitaphs from tombstones. See if you can find a wide variety of examples. (Sad, humorous, biblical, etc.)

Exercise 6

Write an epitaph for yourself. Write it so you can give the reader an insight about your own personality. You can be funny. Or you can be serious. Try one of each.

Exercise 7

Write an epitaph for a famous person. Try to include information about one of the person's achievements in your epitaph.

Census Records

Word List

census: *census*, in Latin, means "to tax." Its original purpose was to provide a way to charge and collect taxes from a government's citizenry.

decennial: occurring or lasting every 10 years

enumerated: counted

extant: still existing

mortality schedules: census records dealing with death information

Census Records

Censuses have been taken at least since biblical times. One of the earliest censuses was ordered by Caesar Augustus during Jesus' time in an attempt to find more sources of tax money and to enforce the military service requirement.

Another early census was the famous *Domesday Book*. The *Domesday Book* was the result of a census ordered by William the Conqueror in 1085 for England. William ordered the census to find out how many people and how much property existed in his newly conquered country. That census produced two massive volumes of names. Beginning in the 1400s, various European cities began to count their populations but the first direct, periodic census began in the United States.

The Constitution mandated Congress to see that the people of the United States were counted every 10 years. This count, considered the first modern census, began in 1790 and has taken place every 10 years since.

Censuses, especially those taken more recently, provide valuable information for the family historian. The accuracy of each census, however, depends almost entirely on the census taker. Unfortunately, over the years and especially in the early censuses, census takers have been guilty of mistakes, oversights and even fictionalizing information. Respondents sometimes deliberately provided wrong information, as well, in misguided efforts to protect their privacy. Despite these shortcomings, census records are still an excellent place to look for information about your family history.

Since the passage of the Right to Privacy Act in 1974, census records have been closed to the public until 72 years after the census is taken. This is to encourage accurate answers from citizens who might not want certain information to become public during their lifetimes. Since it can take up to two years for materials to be microfilmed, it is actually closer to 74 years after a census year for the records to be made available.

1790
Census Schedule

In the 1790 census, about 3.2 million people were counted, not including slaves or untaxed Indians. The results of this census were used as a basis for determining the number of representatives each state would have in the House of Representatives. The information also provided a ready list of men eligible for military service, a much-needed inventory for a brand-new country.

The 1790 census was so simple, only seven questions, that its results provide very little information for the family historian. This census gathered largely generic information: name of the head of a family, the number of free white males 16 or over, the number of free white males under 16, the number of free white females, number of all other free persons and the number of slaves. The only name listed was that of the head of the household.

To make matters worse, much of the 1790 census was destroyed by the British in the War of 1812. Still, there is much to be gleaned from the extant records. And, thankfully, censuses became more detailed and informative after 1790.

1790 Census Form

Place of Enumeration

Page	Name of Head of Family	Free White Males		Free White Females	All other free persons	Slaves	Remarks
		of 16 years and upwards including heads of families	Under 16	Including heads of families			

1790 Census of the United States

1800–1840
Censuses

The censuses from 1800 to 1840 offer only a few more facts to the researcher than the census of 1790. The ages of the household occupants were now grouped into rough divisions, but still the only name listed was the head of the family.

However, by 1820, the government began to use the census schedule to gather additional information. For example, households were required to report any unnaturalized citizens.

The 1820 schedule year also asked for the number of persons engaged in agriculture, commerce and manufacturing. The schedule also asked for the number of free colored persons and slaves and the number of all other persons not taxed, excluding Indians.

The 1840 census was much the same as the 1820 census, with one exception. A special category for the names and ages of those on military pensions was also added.

1800–1810 U.S. Censuses

Original Copy
Extract Copy
Microfilm Copy
Printed Copy

Date of Search

Notes:

Place of Enumeration:

Name of Head of Family	Free White Males					Free White Females					All other free persons except Indians	Slaves	Remarks	Page
	Under 10	10-16	16-26	26-45	45 and over	Under 10	10-16	16-26	26-45	45 and over				

1800-1810 Censuses of the United States

1820 U.S. Census

☐ Original Copy
☐ Extract Copy
☐ Microfilm Copy
☐ Printed Copy

Date of Search _______________________________

Notes:

Place of Enumeration:

Page	Name of Head of Family	Free White Males						Free White Females						Foreigners not naturalized	Agriculture	Commerce	Manufactures	Free Colored	Slaves	Remarks
		Under 10	10-16	16-18	16-26	26-45	45 and over	Under 10	10-16	16-26	26-45	45 and over							

Name____

1830-1840 U.S. Censuses

☐ Original Copy ☐ Extract Copy ☐ Microfilm Copy ☐ Printed Copy

Date of Search____________

Notes:

Place of Enumeration:

Name of Head of Family	Free White Males														Free White Females														Slaves	Free Colored	Foreigners not naturalized	Pensioners (1840 Census Only)	Page
	Under 5	5-10	10-15	15-20	20-30	30-40	40-50	50-60	60-70	70-80	80-90	90-100	Over 100	Under 5	5-10	10-15	15-20	20-30	30-40	40-50	50-60	60-70	70-80	80-90	90-100	Over 100					

1830-1840 Censuses of the United States

1850–1870
Censuses

The census of 1850 was the most significant of the early censuses. For the first time, every member of the household was listed by name. Their relationship to the head of the household was defined. From this census, the family historian can get a picture of free families living together as a unit.

The 1850 and 1860 censuses saw the addition of separate slave schedules. Each slave entry revealed the slave owner's name, but unfortunately, not the name of the slave. However, the entry did ask for the slave's age, sex and color.

The 1870 census format did not change a great deal from that of the 1850-1860 censuses except for one important difference—the slave schedule was omitted, since all slaves had been freed.

1850-1860 U.S. Censuses

Original Copy ☐
Extract Copy ☐
Microfilm Copy ☐
Printed Copy ☐

Date of Search

Notes:

Place of Enumeration:

Page	Dwelling No.	Family No.	Names	Color	Sex	Age prior to June 1st	Month of birth if born in census year	Relationship to head of house	Single	Married	Widowed	Divorced	Married in census year	Occupation	Miscellaneous Information	Cannot read or write	Place of Birth	Place of birth of father	Place of birth of mother	Enumeration Date	Remarks

1850-1860 Censuses of the United States

1880
Census

The 1880 census provides some of the most helpful information for the family historians. That is because this census began to require that both mother's and father's birthplaces be listed. Such information gives the historian a chance to track family origins back to an original source.

Name____

1880 U.S. Census

Place of Enumeration:

Page	Dwelling No.	Family No.	Names	Color	Sex	Age prior to June 1st	Month of birth if born in census yr.	Relationship to head of house	Single	Married	Widowed	Divorced	Married in census year	Occupation	Miscellaneous Information	Cannot read or write	Place of birth	Place of birth of father	Place of birth of mother	Enumeration Date	Remarks

1880 Census of the United States

1890
Census

The 1890 census records were almost completely destroyed by a fire in Washington, D.C., on January 10, 1921. Only partial census records survived. There are census remnants for these states: Alabama, the District of Columbia, Georgia, Illinois, Minnesota, New Jersey, New York, North Carolina, Ohio, South Dakota and Texas.

Sometimes special censuses have been taken. For example, a special census was ordered by the Congress in 1890 to count the Union veterans of the Civil War. Each entry shows a veteran's name. If the veteran was deceased, the name of the surviving spouse was listed.

The veteran's rank, company and regiment or vessel were also given. In addition, the date of enlistment, date of discharge, length of service, postal address and service-connected disabilities also became part of the record.

1900 Census

The 1900 census is important to family historians because this census included the exact birth month and year of everyone counted.

1910 and 1920 Censuses

The 1910 census recorded the number of still-living Civil War veterans and showed an official interest in the handicapped by counting the number of blind, deaf and mute citizens. The 1920 census discontinued the count of Civil War veterans and the handicapped and identified the "mother tongues" of the respondent's mother and father.

The Mortality Schedules

A mortality schedule is simply a record of those who have died during a specified time period. The 1850, 1860, 1870 and 1880 censuses included a special mortality schedule section.

These mortality schedules listed the people who had died during the 12-month period preceding the census. The entries listed age, sex, color, occupation, marital status, place of birth, month of death and cause of death.

Where to Find Census Records

Census records are kept in various places. Many city and state libraries have microfilm copies of the records appropriate for their locality or state. The Latter Day Saints Library in Salt Lake City has copies of all the census material from 1790 to 1920. Copies of this information also can be ordered from the church's branch libraries. The same records are also available in the National Archives in Washington, D.C., as well as in the National Archives' regional offices.

Federal census records were closed to the public until 72 years had passed since the census was taken with the passage of the Right to Privacy Act in 1974.

National Archives
Washington, D.C.

1900 U.S. Census

State _______________________   County _______________________

Page	St. & House No.	Dwelling No.	Family No.	Names	Relationship to head of house	Color	Sex	Date of Birth		Age Last Birthday	Single – Married Widowed – Divorced	No. Yrs. Married
								Mo.	Yr.			

1900 Census of the United States

1900 U.S. Census

Township ___________________ Town ___________________ Ward of City ___________________

Mother No. Child.	No. Child. Living	Place of Birth This Person	Place of Birth Father	Place of Birth Mother	Yr. Immigrate U.S.	No. Yrs. in U.S.	Naturalization	Occupation	Mon. Not Employed	Mon. Attend School	Can Read	Can Write	Can Speak English	Enumeration Date

1900 Census of the United States

Name____

State:		Today's date:														
Country:		Microfilm roll number:														
Parish, Town, District, or City:		(Write addresses above the first name listed in each household.)														

Name	Relation	Personal Description							Education			Ownership of Home			
The name of each person whose place of abode on April 15, 1910, was in this family. Enter surname first, then the given name and middle initial, if any. Include every person living on April 15, 1910. Omit children born since April 15, 1910.	Relationship of each person to the head of this family—whether wife, son, daughter, servant, boarder, or other.	Sex	Color or race	Age at last birthday	Whether single, married, widowed, or divorced	Number of years married	Mother of how many children	Number of children living	Whether able to read	Whether able to write	Attended school any time since September 1, 1909	Owned or rented	Owned free or mortgaged	Farm or house	Number of farm schedule
3	4	5	6	7	8	9	10	11	12	13	14	15	16	17	18

1910 U.S. Census

Nativity. Place of birth of each person and parents of each person enumerated. If born in the United States, give the State or Territory; if of foreign birth, give the Country only.			Citizenship		
Place of Birth of this Person.	Place of Birth of FATHER of this Person.	Place of Birth of MOTHER of this Person.	Year of immigration to the U.S.	Whether naturalized or alien	Whether able to speak English; or if not, give language spoken.
19	20	21	22	23	24

1910 U.S. Census

	Occupation				Whether survivor of the Union or Confederate Army or Navy.	Whether blind (both eyes)	Whether deaf and dumb
Trade or profession of, or particular kind or work done by this person, as spinner, salesman, laborer, etc.	General nature of industry, business, or establishment in which this person works, as cotton mill, dry goods store, farm, etc.	Whether an employer, emplyee or working on own account.	Whether out of work on April 10, 1910, if an employee.	Number of weeks out of work during year 1909 if an employee.			
25	26	27	28	29	30	31	32

Census Summary Chart

Family Name ——

	1790	1800	1810	1820	1830	1840	1850	1860	1870	1880
Husband full name:										
Wife full name:										
Children:										

Summary of Where Family Lived When Census Taken

Census Location

Census Date	
1790	
1800	
1810	
1820	
1830	
1840	
1850	
1860	
1870	
1880	

*1890 census destroyed by fire

Census Review

Exercise 1

1. What is a census? ____

2. How often is the census taken in the United States? ___________________________

3. Why did the U.S. Constitution order a census? ___________________________

____

4. What was the *Domesday Book*? ____

5. Which one of the early censuses is likely to be most helpful to family historians?

____

6. What happened to the 1890 census? ____

7. Which census counted Civil War Union veterans? _______ Which census counted

all living Civil War veterans? _______ How could those censuses be useful?

____

8. What is a mortality schedule? ____

Exercise 2

Research your own family. See if you can identify an early relative who was among those counted in any one of the censuses between 1790 and 1880. You may not be able to identify a relative who lived during this time period. If this is the case, from one of those censuses, select a name at random.

Use the appropriate census form to record all the available information about your relative or the person whom you randomly selected. Notice how much information about a family the federal census contains. These activities will help you to understand how useful census records can be in providing information about your early family history.

Exercise 3

If you can, track a family through several decades. Record the results on the Census Summary Chart on page 94.

Name____

Neigborhood Census

Exercise 4

Here is a sample neighborhood census form you can use to take a mini census in your own neighborhood. (Be sure the household you are calling on knows why you are requesting the information.)

Interview an adult member of the household whenever possible, and record the results of your findings. Can you see differences between people in the same neighborhood, even though your neighbors seem to be quite a bit alike?

Think about a person taking the census in 1790. What problems would a census taker have encountered? What problems do census takers run into today?

SAMPLE NEGHBORHOOD FORM

Neigborgood or street ____

NAME	HOUSE NUMB.	# OF YRS LIVED ON THE BLOCK	# OF PEOPLE LIVING IN H.	# CARS	# OF PETS AND KIND	# TV	OCCUPATION(S) OF ADULT(S)

Immigration

Word List

emigration: to leave a country

immigration: to enter a country

indentured servant: a person under a contract of service to another person for a period of years, usually three to seven

naturalization: legal change of citizenship from one country to another country

The United States has long been the world's number one destination for immigration. For almost 400 years it has served as a symbol of new beginnings and opportunity.

The first immigrants to settle the eastern American seaboard were English. In 1607, an English expedition led by John Smith settled in Jamestown, Virginia, and in 1620, the Pilgrims landed at Plymouth Rock, Massachusetts.

Many of the early immigrants came for religious reasons. The Puritans and the Quakers, for example, fled from England because they disagreed with the doctrines of the Church of England. The Huguenots, French Protestants, left their native land because they suffered persecution by Catholics.

But many others came for economic reasons—for land, for the promise of riches and independence. But in an effort to obtain that independence, some of these early immigrants had to come to America as indentured servants. In return for their passage, these immigrants agreed to work for a period of time, usually three to seven years. Children in indentured families usually were sold to the highest bidder and generally remained in servitude until the age of 21. Many families sold one or two of their children to raise money.

Still, indentured servants had a choice. In 1619, 20 Africans were bonded into slavery in the colonies and a disastrous precedent was set that would only be ended by a terrible fratricidal war two-and-a-half centuries later. By 1808, when Congress finally outlawed the importation of new slaves, about 375,000 Africans had been forcibly brought to this new land, mostly from western Africa. Another 50,000 English convicts from England were forced to the colonies in the 1700s.

Other
immigrants traveled to
this country because of war,
political turmoil or economic crises in their
home countries. The 1845-1847 Irish potato
famine, for example, forced millions of people facing
starvation to leave their homeland. More recently, war in
Vietnam, poverty in Mexico and the Philippines and the
political systems of Cuba and China have propelled waves of
immigrants to America.

All told, the United States has accepted considerably more immigrants than any other country in the world. Since 1820, more than 50 million people have moved to America and become citizens.

The best sources for family historians looking for information about immigrants in the 19th century and the first half of the 20th century are passenger lists and naturalization records.

Passenger lists are manifests—or records—kept by the captain of a ship. The lists include the name of each passenger, the name of the passenger's country, departure point and destination.

Unfortunately, many of these early records are missing and still others were poorly maintained, now damaged or illegible. However, there are still a good many passenger lists available, and these lists can turn up helpful clues to family origins.

Records of these lists, in large part, are housed at the National Archives. The records in the National Archives go back as far as 1798, but the bulk of them are for the years 1820 to 1919.

Some of the records are more recent—as recent as 1945, in fact. Most records after 1945 are kept at the U.S. Department of Immigration and Naturalization.

The National Archives will search for names of persons on their passenger lists, if provided with the following information:

1. the passenger's full name

2. the port (city) of entry

3. the date of entry (as close as possible)

4. the name of the ship, if known.

Naturalization records are also valuable sources of information. These records are kept at the Immigration and Naturalization Service, 119 D Street, N.W., Washington, D.C. 20536.

Maps

The United States map has
changed a great deal since the signing
of the Declaration of Independence. The
nation has grown from a tiny band of 13 colonies
huddled on the Atlantic coast to a nation of 50 states
sprawling across a continent and beyond. The nation
began to push its boundaries west soon after its birth as
various land acquisitions launched the opening of new territories.
As fast as the land could be acquired (and even before), restless
Americans started the trek west across the Appalachians to the new
frontier.

The first major territorial acquisition—the Northwest Territory in 1783—made it necessary for the United States to establish a consistent method for settling these new lands. The result was the Ordinance of 1785, which provided for the orderly political division of the land.

The territory was first surveyed into six-mile-square townships. Each township, in turn, was divided into 36 equal sections. Each section was made up of 640 acres. Then the government auctioned the land to settlers. The land was usually offered on a first-come, first-served basis, often for less than a dollar an acre. These provisions of the ordinance set a precedent for the fair and orderly settlement of each new territory.

Another Northwest Ordinance followed in 1787 and established the rules about how the territory was to be governed. Under this ordinance, it was possible for these new territories to take the steps that would bring them statehood. A population of 5000 adult males qualified the territory to elect its own legislature.

Finally, the territory was eligible for statehood when its population reached 60,000. Large territories often became several states. The Northwest Territory, for instance, was eventually divided into the states of Wisconsin, Michigan, Illinois, Indiana, Ohio and part of Minnesota.

Locating
Records

There were few, if any, town or city records
in these new territories and states for the simple
fact that there were no towns or cities. The early
populations were just too small and spread out. Thus, the
county governments were the only entities keeping records.
But the populations were in great flux, understandably. More
people arrived. Population centers shifted, expanded or disappeared.
The counties moved, grew or divided in response. This raises a great
challenge for the family researcher seeking county records for his
ancestors.

For example, Randolph County, Illinois, was once a large county in the Northwest Territory. By 1831, however, Randolph County had been divided to form a new, smaller Randolph County and eight other new counties—Gallatin, Edwards, Crawford, Clark, Pike, Fulton, Putnam and Cook.

After the divisions, some of the records which were once stored in the Randolph County Courthouse may have been moved to one of eight new courthouses. A map of the original Randolph County could help you discern which courthouse now holds the records.

Randolph County is by no means the only county to have such a confusing history. Towns, too, have been moved from one county to another, or even shifted to a new state! Clearly, under these all-too-common circumstances, an early map becomes vital to the historian who is searching for the elusive courthouse containing his or her family records. Libraries, with their early atlas and map collections, are a great place to begin that search.

When researching county histories and county vital records, be sure to discover if the records sought actually reside in the county being researched. County borders changed drastically as states grew. Review the maps of Pennsylvania on pages 101 and 102 to see how county boundaries changed over time.

Pennsylvania Maps

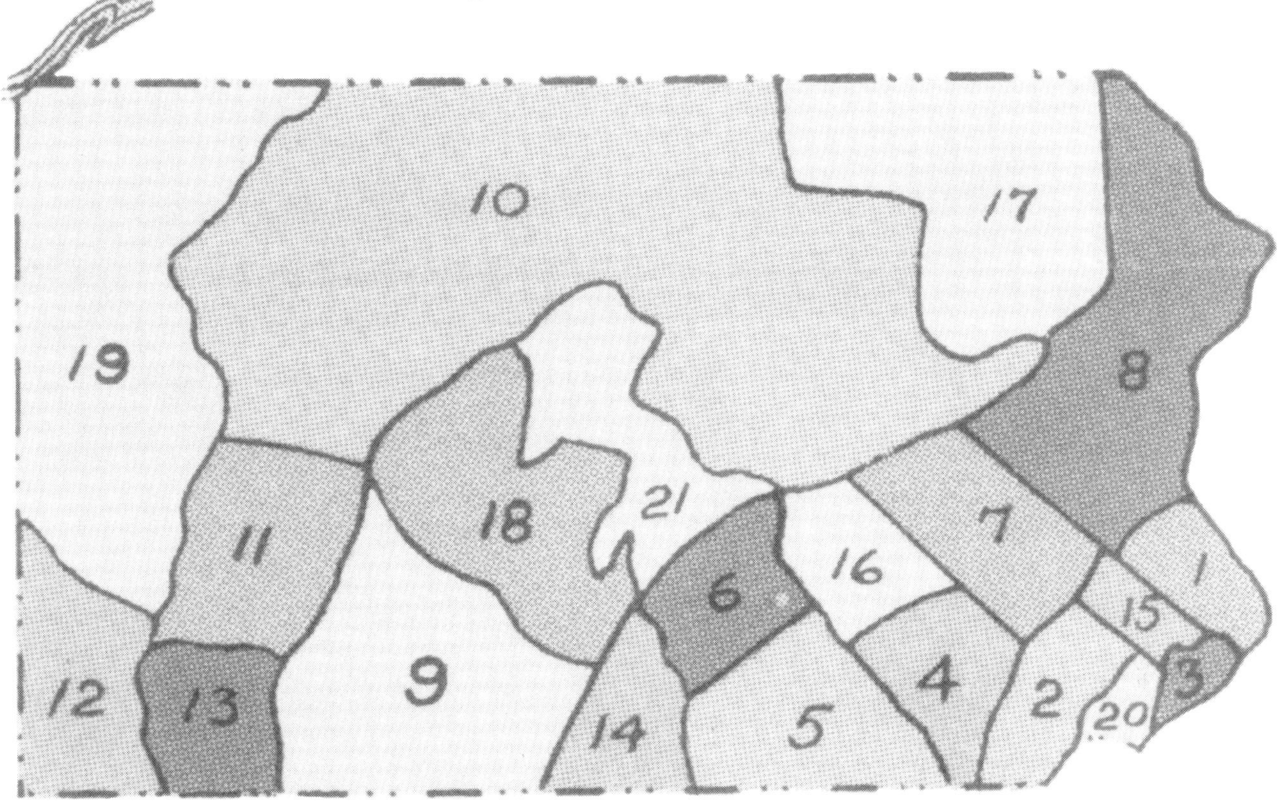

21 Counties, 1790

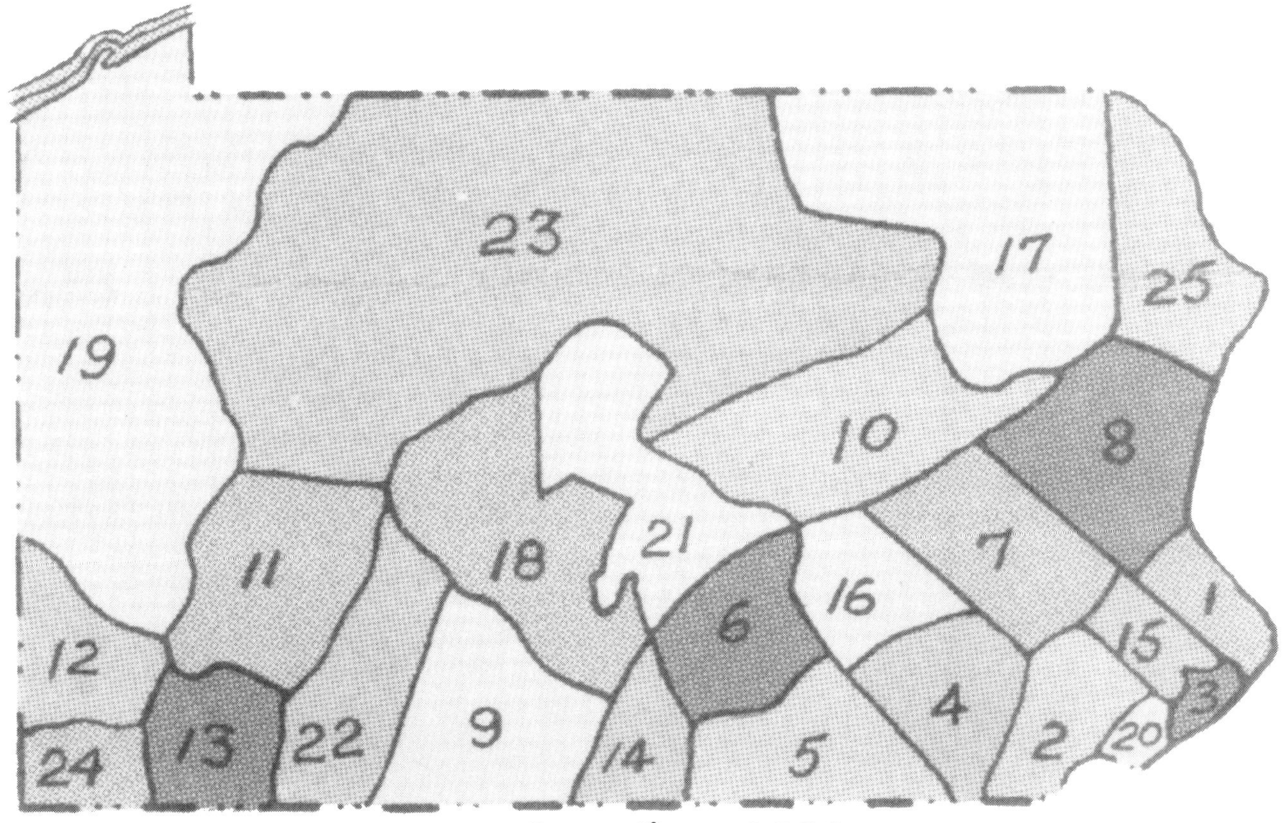

25 Counties, 1800

Pennsylvania Maps

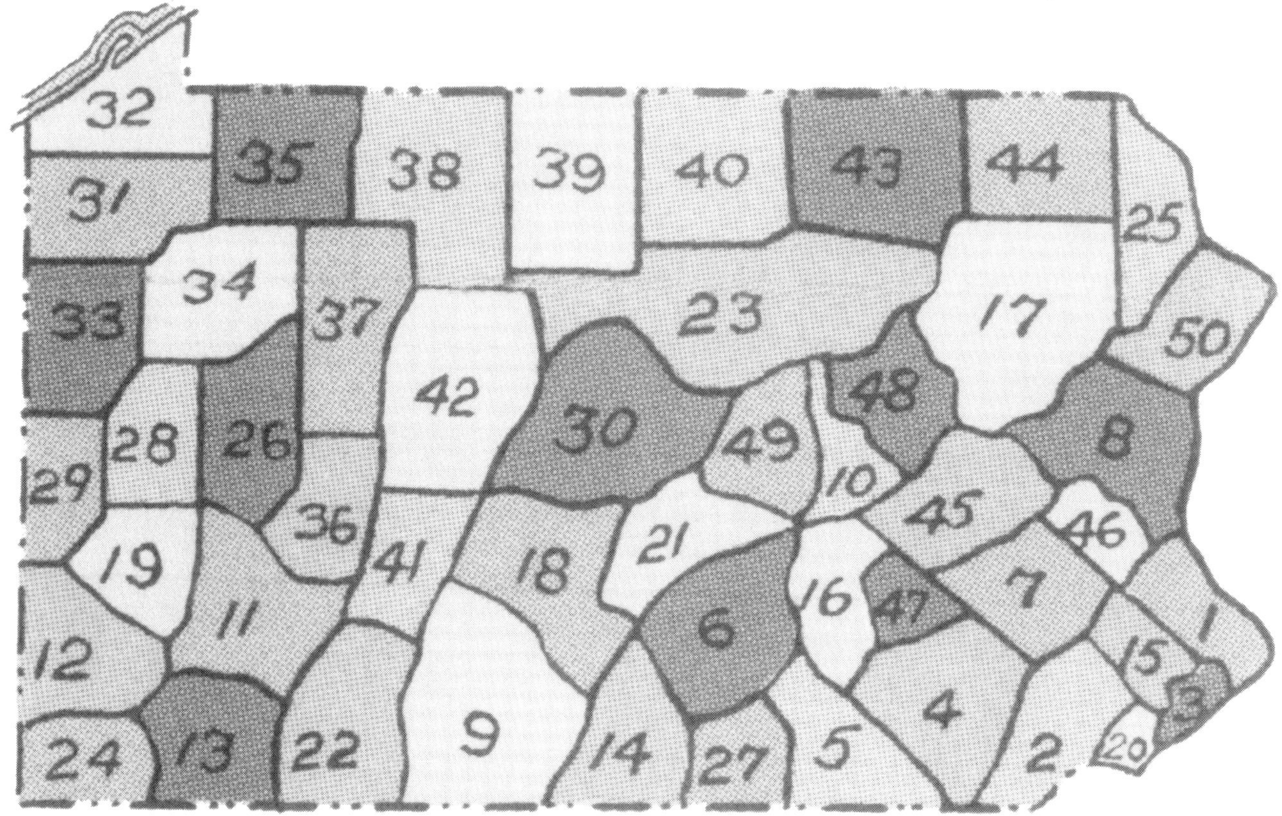

50 Counties, 1820

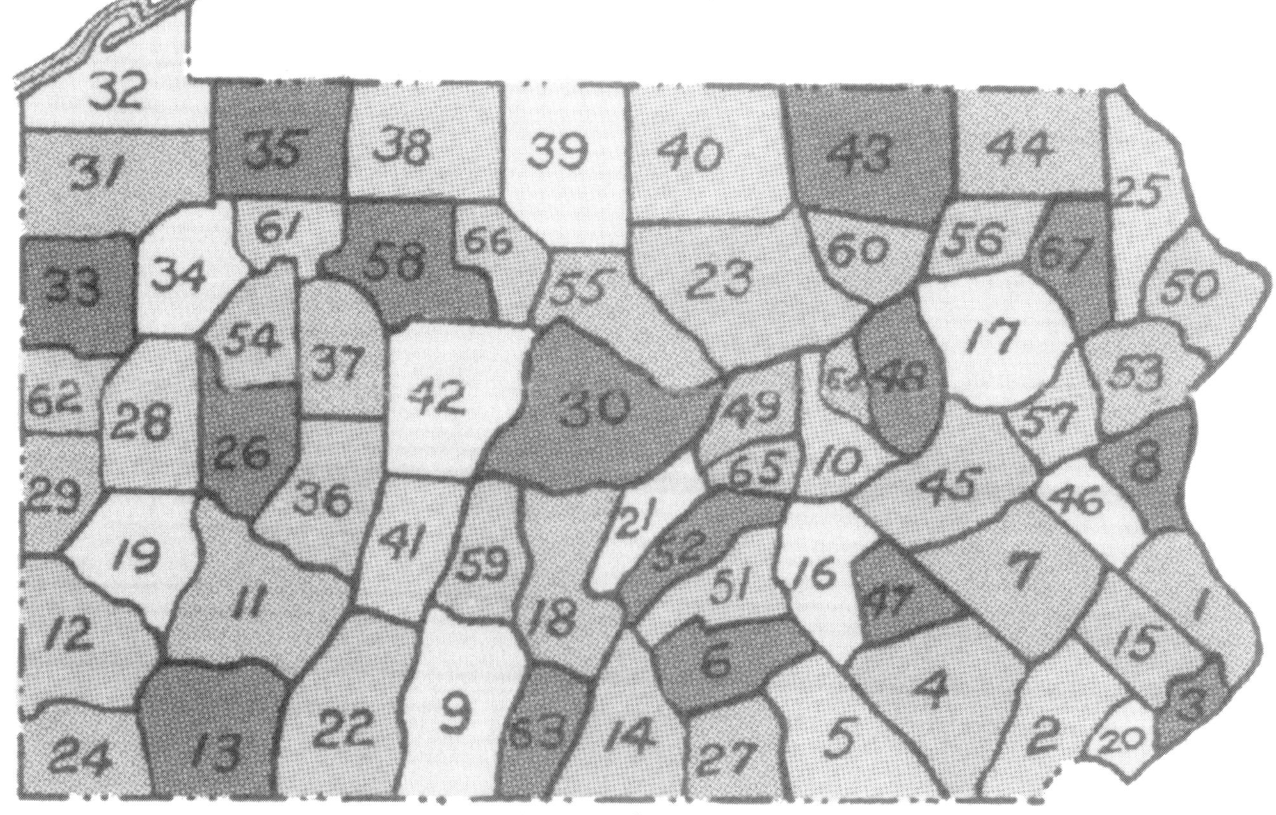

67 Counties, 1932

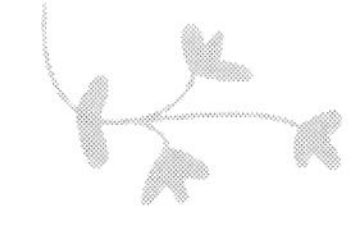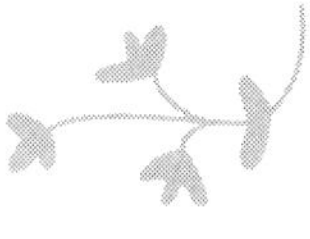

Map Review

Exercise 1

1. In what township do you live? _______________________________________

2. In what county do you live? ____

3. What is the county seat of your county? _______________________________

4. When was your state admitted to the Union? ___________________________

5. Was your state ever part of a territory? If so, what territory? _____________

Exercise 2

Below is a map of some former United States territories. Write the letter of the year that the territory became part of the U.S.

_______ 1. Mexican Cession   a. 1803

_______ 2. Oregon Country   b. 1819

_______ 3. Louisiana Purchase   c. 1845

_______ 4. Texas Annexation   d. 1846

_______ 5. Florida Purchase   e. 1848

World Map

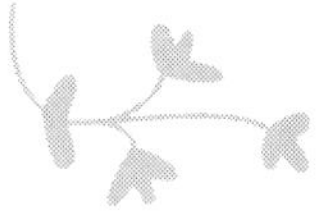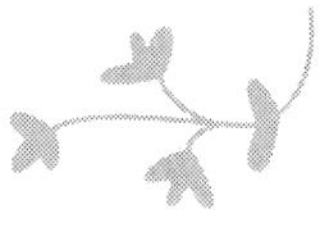

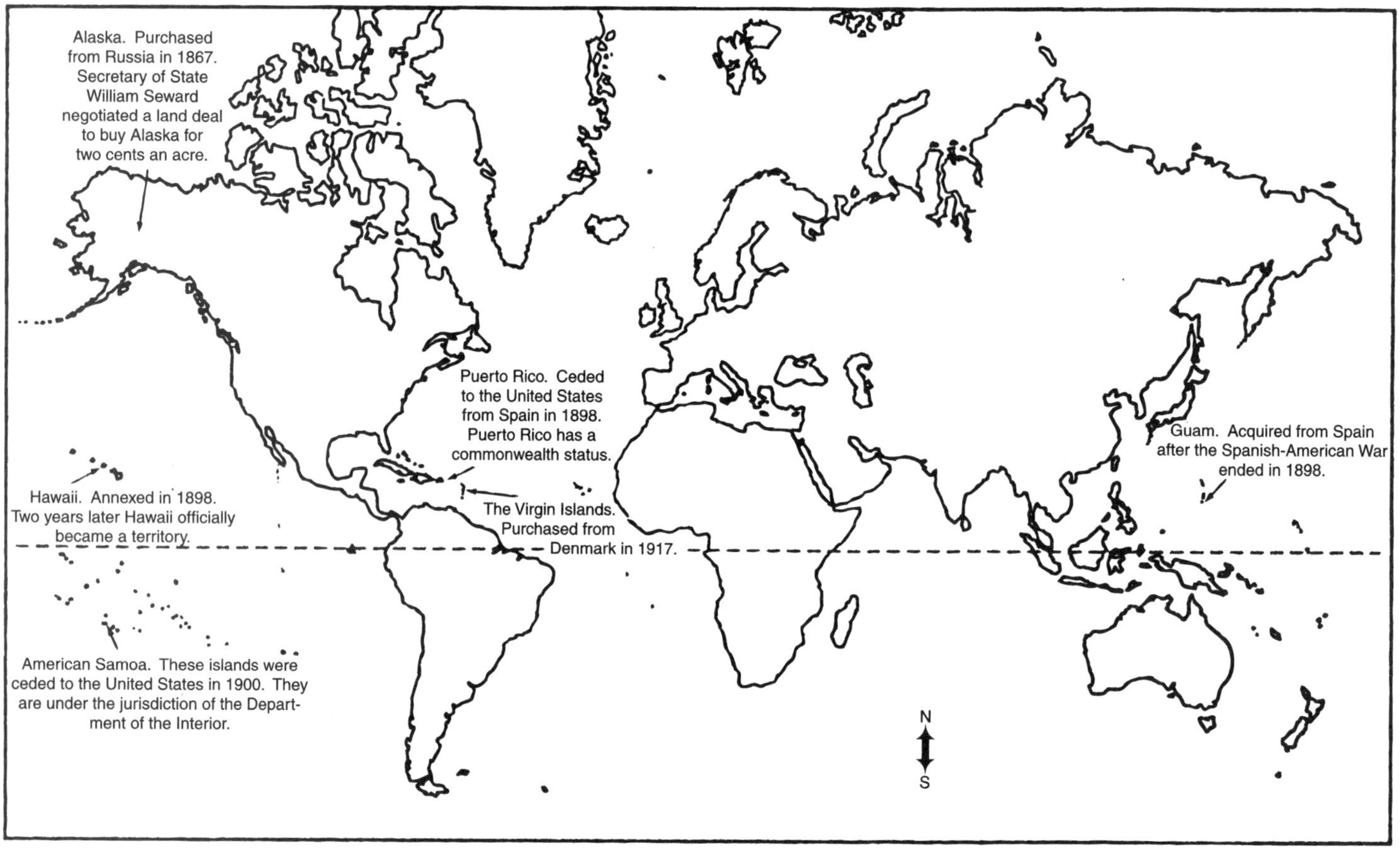

Exercise 3

Here is a map of some former United States territories. Write the letter of the year that each tract became a United States territory. Some of the letters will be used more than once.

_______ 1. Guam   a. 1867

_______ 2. Samoa   b. 1898

_______ 3. Puerto Rico   c. 1900

_______ 4. Virgin Islands   d. 1917

_______ 5. Hawaii

_______ 6. Alaska

Wills

Word List

administrator: a person appointed by the court to settle the estate of a deceased person (administratrix, if female)

executor: a person named in a will to carry out the provisions of that will (executrix, if female)

heir: a person who inherits property, personal effects or money from someone who has died

holographic will: a handwritten will

intestate: dying without a will

nuncupative will: a will given orally in front of witnesses and then written down

testate: dying with a will

testator: a person who dies with a will in force (testatrix, if female)

will: a legal document that directs the distribution of one's property after death

Wills contain a great deal of interesting and valuable information for the family historian. Several generations may be mentioned in a single will. The information revealed in these wills often enables the historian to piece together family relationships.

The wills themselves can be written in mind-boggling legal language, but they can also be scratched out in simple words on a scrap of paper. Both versions are just as legal and binding.

The laws affecting wills are complicated. Although probate laws can vary from state to state, the general format of wills is the same throughout the United States. Aside from the legal language, wills are generally straightforward. They include, of course, the name and address of the person writing the will. This person is known as the testator.

The testator lists the heirs. These are the persons who are to receive the testator's money, property or personal effects. Most often these heirs are relatives. In most states, a living spouse must receive some portion of the inheritance. In Louisiana, the children are entitled to an inheritance by law. The heirs, however, can be friends, charitable organizations, museums, schools or even a favorite pet.

An executor is also named in
the will. This person is charged with
fulfilling the instructions of the will.
Sometimes, the executor cannot, or will not, accept
that duty. The executor is then said to renounce the
task. If this happens, the court appoints an administrator to
see that the provisions of the will are carried out.

Somewhere in the will, usually near the end, the testator declares all other wills void. Finally, the date and signature are affixed, along with the signatures of witnesses. Some wills also outline burial plans and include last words to heirs.

Most wills are written and prepared with the aid of an attorney. But sometimes a person will dictate to someone else the conditions of the will. This often happens when the person is gravely ill or has been critically injured in an accident. These so-called "deathbed" wills are more accurately termed nuncupative wills.

Many people die without any will at all. A person who dies without a will is said to be intestate. State laws vary on how property is to be divided when there is no will. Some states give one-third to the spouse and two-thirds to the children. These decisions are made in probate courts. The results of these decisions are usually recorded in the deceased's county of residence.

On the following page is the last Will and Testament of John Howland, 1672.

Last
Will & Testament of
John Howland, 1672

*The Last Will and Testament of mr John howland of Plymouth late
Deceased, exhibited to the Court held att Plymouth the fift Day of March Anno
Dom 1672 on the oathes of mr Samuell ffuller and mr William Crow as followeth*

*Know all men to whom these prsents shall Come That I John howland senir of the Towne of
New Plymouth in the Collonie of New Plymouth in New England in America, this twenty ninth
Day of May one thousand six hundred seaventy and two being of whole mind, and in Good and prfect
memory and Remembrance praised be God: being now Grown aged; haveing many Infeirmities, of body
upon mee; and not Knowing how soon God will call mee out of this world, Doe make and ordaine these
prsents to be my Testament Containing herein my last Will in manor and forme following;*

*I Will and bequeath my body to the Dust and my soule to God that Gave it in hopes of a Joyfull Resurrection unto
Glory; and as Concerning my temporall estate, I Dispose thereof as followeth;*

*Item I Doe give and bequeath unto John howland my eldest sonne besides what lands I have alreddy given him, all My
Right and Interest To that one hundred acres of land graunted mee by the Court lying on the eastern side of Tauton
River; between Teticutt and Taunton bounds and all the appurtenances and privilidges Therunto belonging, T belonge to
him and his heirs and assignes for ever; and if that Tract should faile, then to have all my Right title and, Interest by and
in that Last Court graunt to mee in any other place, To belonge to him his heires and assignes forever;*

*Item I give and bequeath unto my son Jabez howland all those my upland and Meadow That I now posesse at Satuckett
and Paomett, and places adjacent, with all the, appurtenances and privilidges, belonging. therunto, and all my right title
and Interest therin, To belonge to him his heires and assignes for ever,*

*Item I Give and bequeath unto my son Jabez howland all that my one peece of land that I have lying on the southsyde of
the Mill brooke, in the Towne of Plymouth aforsaid; be it more or lesse; and is on the Northsyde of a feild that is now
Gyles Rickards senir To belonge to the said Jabez his heirs and assignes for ever;*

*Item I give and bequeath unto Isacke howland my youngest sonne all those my uplands and meddows Devided
and undivided with all the appurtenances and priviliges unto them belonging, lying and being in the Towne of
Middlebery, and in a tract of Land Called the Majors, Purchase, near Namassakett, Ponds; which I have
bought and purchased of William White of Marshfeild in the Collonie of New Plymouth; which may or
shall appeer by any Deed or writinges Together with the aformentioned prticulares To belonge to the
said Isacke his heirs and assignes for ever;*

*Item I give and bequeath unto my said son Isacke howland the one halfe of my twelve acree
lott of Meddow. That I now have att Winnatucsett River within the Towne of
Plymouth aforsaid To belonge to him and said Isacke howland his heires and
assignes for ever,*

*Item I Will and bequeath unto My Deare and loveing wife
Elizabeth howland the use and benifitt of my now
Dwelling house in Rockey nooke in*

the Township of Plymouth aforsaid,
with the outhousing lands, That is uplands
uplands [sic] and meddow lands and all appurtenances, and
privilidges therunto belonging in the Towne of Plymouth and all other
Lands housing and meddowes that I have in the said Towne of Plymouth
excepting what meddow and upland I have before given To my sonnes Jabez and
Isacke howland During her naturall life to Injoy make use of and Improve for her benifitt
and Comfort;

Item I give and bequeath unto my son Joseph howland after the Decease of my loveing wife Elizabeth
howland my aforsaid Dwelling house att Rockey nooke together with all the outhousing uplands and
Medowes appurtenances and privilidges belonging therunto; and all other housing uplands and meddowes
appurtenances and privilidges That I have within the aforsaid Towne of New Plymouth excepting what lands
and meadowes I have before Given To my two sonnes Jabez and Isacke; To belong to him the said Joseph howland
To him and his heire's and assignes for ever;

Item I give and bequeath unto my Daughter Desire Gorum twenty shillings

Item I give and bequeath To my Daughter hope Chipman twenty shillings

Item I give, and bequeath unto my Daughter Elizabeth Dickenson twenty shillings

Item I give and bequeath unto my Daughter Lydia Browne twenty shillings

Item I give & bequeath to my Daughter hannah Bosworth twenty shillings

Item I give and bequeath unto my Daughter Ruth Cushman twenty shillings

Item I give to my Grandchild Elizabeth howland The Daughter of my son John howland twenty shillings

Item my will is That these legacyes Given to my Daughters, be payed by my exequitrix in such species as shee thinketh
meet;

Item I will and bequeath unto my loveing wife Elizabeth howland, my Debts and legacyes being first payed my whole
estate: vis: lands houses goods Chattles; or any thing else that belongeth or appertaineth unto mee, undisposed of be
it either in Plymouth Duxburrow or Middlbery or any other place whatsoever; I Doe freely and absolutly give and
bequeath it all to my Deare and loveing wife Elizabeth howland whom I Doe by these prsents, make ordaine
and Constitute to be the sole exequitrix of this my Last will and Testament to see the same truely and
faithfully prformed according to the tenour therof; In witness whereof I the said John howland senir
have heerunto sett my hand and seale the aforsaid twenty ninth Day of May, one thousand six
hundred seaventy and two 1672

Signed and sealed in the prsence of Samuel ffuller John Howland

William Crow And a seale

Wills

The following will was written February 3, 1881. It is a nuncupative will. Ezra Vincent, the man who dictated the will, was 73 years old at the time and seriously ill. He was too weak to do any more than sign his name. Two days later, he died.

Here is the text of Mr. Vincent's will. Can you see how wills can be helpful for the family historian? In this case, you can see how the will helps define the relationship between the testator and the heirs.

I, EZRA VINCENT, of State of Iowa, Harrison County, do hereby ordain and declare this to be my last will and testament. After all my lawful debts are paid, I devise and bequeath all my property both personal and real to be divided as follows:

To my daughter, Julia Shepard, I bequeath the sum of three hundred dollars ($300). She and her husband already having had considerable advanced in the way of provision and groceries.

To my daughter, Emma Reagor, I bequeath three hundred and fifty dollars ($350) and one feather bed.

To my son, Hiram G. Vincent, I bequeath the sum of three hundred and fifty dollars ($350).

To my daughter, Viola M. Hardy, I bequeath one bed, one bureau, one horse, the bay mare, now in possession of her husband, S.T. Hardy and one thousand dollars ($1000).

To my son, James Ezra Vincent, I bequeath the sum of eight hundred dollars ($800).

To my son, Jonathan Vincent, I bequeath the sum of eight hundred dollars ($800).

The residue of my estate if any after paying the several amounts herein before mentioned to be divided equally among my children.

I hereby appoint Jonathan Vincent and S.T. Hardy, executors of this will.

I hereby revoke all other wills.

In witness whereof I have signed and published this instrument to be my last will and testament, signed and executed this third day of February, A.D. 1881.

Ezra Vincent [signature]

The foregoing instrument was at the date thereof subscribed by Ezra Vincent in our presence, and he at same time declared the same to be his last will and testament and by his request we signed our names thereto as witnesses both in his presence and in presence of each other.

H.H. Roadifer   N.B. Hardy   [signatures of will witnesses]

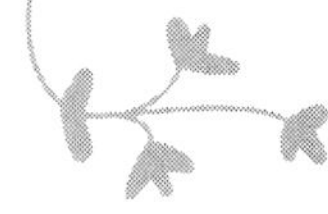 # Will Review 

Exercise 1

Answer the following questions about Ezra Vincent's will:

1. Who is the testator of the will? ____

2. Who served as executors? ____

3. How is S.T. Hardy related to Ezra Vincent? ____

4. Who were H.H. Roadifer and N.B. Hardy? ____

   ____

5. What did Ezra Vincent leave to his daughter Viola? ____

   ____

6. How might Ezra Vincent's will be helpful to a family historian? ____

   ____

Exercise 2

Not everyone can write a legal will. Persons under legal age, for example, cannot write a will. Legal age varies from state to state. In some states, the legal age is 21. In other states, the age is as low as 18. Let's assume, however, that you are of legal age. Write a will using Mr. Vincent's will as a guide.

Heraldry

Word List

coat of arms: a design used to represent individual families

crusader: a European soldier who fought in one of the religious wars in the Middle East in the 12th and 13th centuries

knight: a man given an honorable military rank and sworn to chivalrous conduct in medieval times

During the Crusades, soldiers on the battlefield wore heavy armor for protection. It covered their entire bodies, including their faces, leaving them unrecognizable to their fellow soldiers. Men in the ranks were unable to find their leaders and confusion quickly ensued.

This made it necessary for knights to create and display a highly visible identifying mark or insignia.

During the 1300s, these identifying marks became increasingly more elaborate in their design. The decorations eventually covered the shields of the knights. However, in the heat of battle, shields were not always easy to see and were prone to being dropped so ornaments were also mounted on helmets and copies of these ornaments, called crests, were sewn on surcoats. These surcoats, colorful robes worn over armor, then literally became coats of arms.

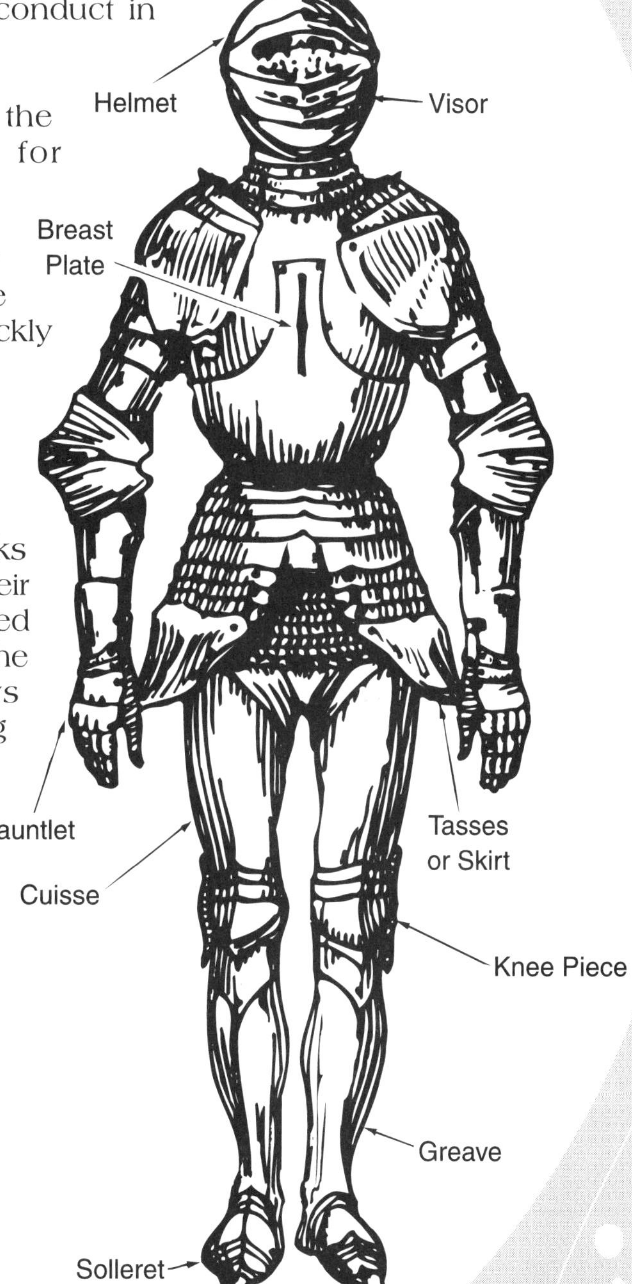

Knights sometimes battled each other over the rights to use a coat of arms design. To stop the bickering, Henry V of England, early in the 15th century, forbade anyone from adopting a coat of arms unless the design was inherited or given by the crown.

In 1484, Richard III established the College of Arms. The college was made up of heralds, men who memorized the different coats of arms of knights, and settled disputes over which knight had the legal right to a coat of arms design.

These designs came to represent more than the knight himself but his entire family and its history, as well. The coats of arms displayed features symbolizing anything from past heroic feats to a family trade to the supposed inherited attributes of a family line. Everything meant something, even the colors of the background had deeper meaning.

The elements of a coat of arms included:

The Motto

A motto was a choice of words found on the coat of arms. A motto might have included words of hope, philosophy or it might have simply provided information. Some coats of arms had no motto, while others had one or more. The motto was usually displayed in a ribbon below the shield.

The Shield

The shield, or escutcheon, was the most important part of a coat of arms. The shield was made up of the field and the charges.

The Field

The field was the surface of the shield, or the background, where the design and charges were placed. The field could be divided in a variety of ways, in as many as nine sections, but for the activity at the end of this chapter, the field is "quartered," or divided into fourths.

The Colors

The colors used carried specific meanings. Here are a few of the traditional representations:

gold—generosity
silver—peace and honesty
red—brave, strong and just
blue—truth and loyalty
green—hope, joy and love
black—dependability

Interestingly, reddish-purple and orange were considered to be colors of disgrace.

The
Charges

Charges were figures, flowers, animals, monsters, people, natural and manmade objects that were placed on the field. The symbolism of some charges are obvious. For instance, a hammer might represent a family of carpenters while a ship would signify a sea-faring family. A book could mean a scholar or teacher while a plow would symbolize a farming family. The meanings of other symbols are less apparent today. Here are some of the more common charges used and their meanings:

bear—strength and cunning

bee—industrious; hardworking

camel—patience and perseverance

castle—safety

dragon—valor and protection

eagle—nobility and strength

faming heart—intense, burning affection

hand—sincerity and faith

hawk—one who does not rest until goal is reached

lightning bolt—swiftness and power

lion—dauntless courage

rainbow—good times after bad

red rose—grace and beauty

scallop shell—a great traveller

snake—wisdom

swan—poetry and learning

sword—justice and honor

white rose—faith and love

unicorn—extreme courage

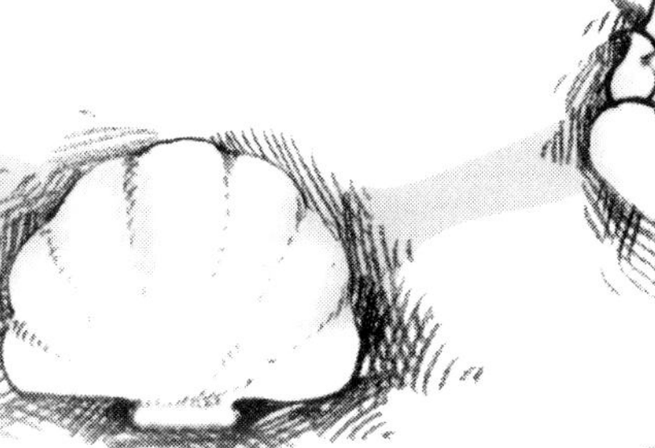

 Coat of Arms 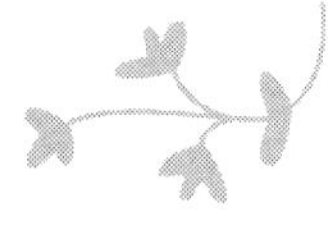

Exercise 1

Design your own family coat of arms on the quartered shield. Be sure to include a motto. You may use any of the symbols presented or make up your own to represent not only you, but your parents, grandparents or other ancestors. Consider occupations, hobbies, family stories and traits for ideas.

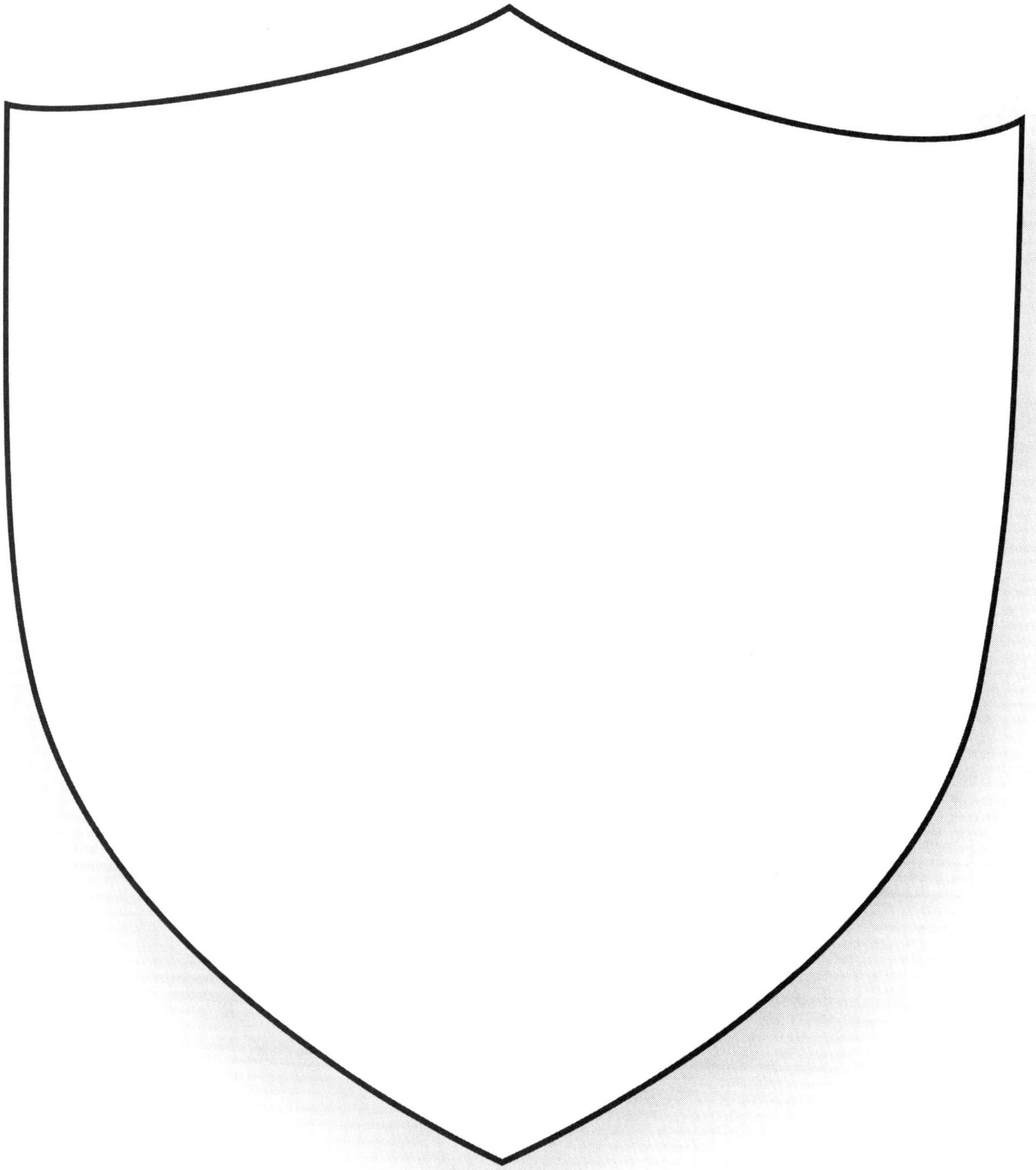

Vital Statistics

The records of such events as births, marriages and deaths are commonly referred to as vital statistics. These records are good primary sources of information, although the amount of information available varies widely from place to place and from century to century.

Births, marriages and deaths are usually recorded where the event took place. For example, if a couple was married in Levittown, Pennsylvania, a record of the marriage could most likely be found at the Bucks County Courthouse in Doylestown, Pennsylvania.

Because Pennsylvania marriage records have been centralized, a record of the same marriage could also be found at the Division of Vital Statistics in New Castle, Pennsylvania.

Each
of the 50 states varies as
to when it began centralizing
records of vital statistics. New Hampshire,
for example, started keeping birth, death and
marriage records as early as 1640.

On the other hand, some states have begun only relatively recently to gather records in a central location. As a matter of fact, it was not until January 1941, that the state of Pennsylvania began maintaining centralized marriage records.

Since record keeping practices vary widely among the states, it's important to know in what state, and, preferably, in what city or town the event being researched took place.

Once the site of the event is known, the procedures to follow become clear. Two pamphlets published by the United States Government Printing Office can be of great benefit in a search:

Where to Write for Marriage Records,
United States and Outlying Areas

and

Where to Write for Birth and Death
Records, United States and Outlying Areas

These pamphlets can be ordered from the U.S. Government Printing Office, Superintendent of Documents, Washington, D.C. 20402.

Most states did not begin keeping vital statistics records until around the turn of the 19th century. For earlier birth-death records, especially in New England, the best source is frequently the town clerk in the town or township where the event took place.

When writing for marriage records, it is important to include as much information as possible. The more complete the information, the more complete the response is likely to be.

For example, in a search for
confirmation of marriage information, a
query letter should contain as much of the
following information as possible:

1. full name of bride

2. full name of groom (Include nicknames. Often, especially
   in older records, a nickname was listed instead of a given
   name.)

3. place of residence

4. ages at the time of the marriage or dates of birth

5. place of marriage

6. the month, day and year of the marriage

7. how information will be used

8. correspondent's relationship to the bride and groom

When writing for a birth or death record,
include all of the following information, if known:

1. full name of person

2. sex and race

3. parents' names, mother's maiden name

4. month, day, year of birth or death

5. place of birth or death (city or town, county and state)

6. how information will be used

7. correspondent's relationship to the person whose record is being
   requested

Be aware that the character and format of the records, as well as the amount
of information that may be forthcoming, can vary widely.

Name____

Sample Birth Certificate

Place of Birth

County _______________________________

City or Town _______________________________

Name of Hosp. or Inst. _______________________________

____

Usual Residence of Mother

State _________ County_______________________

City or Town _______________________________

Street Address _______________________________

Child's Full Name _______________________________

____

Sex _______________________________

This birth single ________ twin ________ triplet ________

If twin or triplet, 1st ________ 2nd ________ 3rd ________

Date and Hour of Birth_______________________________

Father of Child

____
First   Middle   Last

Age _______________________________

Birthplace _______________________________

Usual Occupation _______________________________

Mother of child–Full Name
Including Maiden Name

____
First   Middle   Maiden

Last

Age _______________________________

Birthplace _______________________________

Number of children previously
born to this mother_______________________________

Informant

____

Attnedant's Name _______________________________

Attendant at Birth _______________________________

M.D. _____ D.O. _____ Other _______________________________

Attendant's Address

____

____

Date Signed _______________________________

Date Rec'd by Local Reg. _______________________________

Local Registrar's Name _______________________________

Birth Number Assigned by State Officer

____

118

Name____

Sample Marriage Certificate

Place of Marriage

State of ____

County of____

Township of ____

Town or City of ____

| GROOM | BRIDE |

Full Name_________________________________ | Full Name_________________________________

Residence ________________________________ | Residence ________________________________

Age ______________________________________ | Age ______________________________________

Birthdate_________________________________ | Birthdate_________________________________

Birthplace ________________________________ | Birthplace ________________________________

Occupation _______________________________ | Occupation _______________________________

Name of Father
   or Guardian ___________________________ | Name of Father
   or Guardian ___________________________

Birthplace ________________________________ | Birthplace ________________________________

Maiden Name of Mother ___________________ | Maiden Name of Mother ___________________

Birthplace________________________________ | Birthplace________________________________

If a Minor, Name of Person Consenting for | If a Minor, Name of Person Consenting for

____ | ____

Date of License ______________________________________

License Number ______________________________________

Date of Marriage _____________________________________

By Whom the
Marriage Was
Performed ____

Name ____

Sample Death Certificate

<table>
<tr><td>PLACE OF DEATH</td><td>USUAL RESIDENCE OF DECEASED</td></tr>
<tr><td>County _______________________</td><td>State _______________________</td></tr>
<tr><td>Township _______________________</td><td>County _______________________</td></tr>
<tr><td>City or Town _______________________</td><td>City or Town _______________________</td></tr>
<tr><td>Hospital or Institution _______________________</td><td>Street No. _______________________</td></tr>
<tr><td>Address _______________________</td><td>Citizen of Foreign Country _______________________</td></tr>
<tr><td>Length of Stay in Hosp. _______________________</td><td>Name of Country _______________________</td></tr>
</table>

FULL NAME OF DECEASED ____

Sex _______________ Color _______________ Marital Status _______________________

Name of Spouse _______________________ Age (if alive) _______________

Birth Date of Deceased _______________________ Age at Death _______________

Birthplace ____

Usual Occupation _______________________ Industry or Business _______________________

Father's Name _______________________ Birthplace _______________________

Mother's Name _______________________ Birthplace _______________________

Informant _______________________ Address _______________________

Burial, Cremation, Removal _______________________ Date _______________

Place of Burial or Cremation _______________________ Location _______________

Funeral Director _______________________ Address _______________

Local Registrar _______________________ District _______________ Rec'd _______________

Date of Death _______________ Cause _______________ Physician _______________

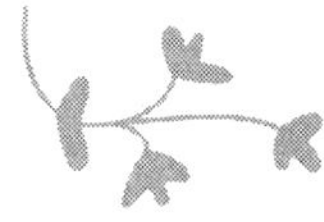 # *Vital Statistics* 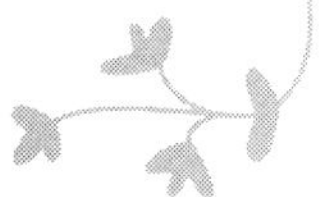

Exercise 1

1. What are vital statistics? ____

____

2. Are vital statistic records considered primary information sources for research?

____

3. Where should you write to obtain a copy of a birth certificate? ____________

____

Exercise 2

Complete the sample birth certificate (page 118) with information about your own birth. Do not use any documents. Instead, ask your parents to help you provide the details you aren't able to come up with. If neither parent is available, perhaps a close relative could help you. Compare your finished copy of the sample with your original birth certificate, if it is available. Are there any differences?

Exercise 3

Complete the sample marriage certificate (page 119) using your parents' marriage as a model. Do not use any documents. Instead, ask your parents to provide you the details that you don't have. Compare your finished copy of the sample marriage certificate with the original certificate. Are there any differences?

Exercise 4

Complete the sample death certificate (page 120) with information about someone you know who has died. Do not use any documents. Instead, seek information from a person or people who knew the deceased. Compare your finished sample certificate with the original death certificate. Are there any differences? (Caution: Please be mindful of people's feelings of grief. It is best not to interview a person about a recent death.)

Newspapers

TRAGEDY AT MODALE

Automobile Struck by Passenger Train, Two Instantly Killed, Two Others Died Later.

Friday evening of last week while "Casey Jones" was coming down the Northwestern track near Modale, in the mist and rain, an automobile driven by "Col" Thompson, was running down the highway towards the same destination. This car contained five passengers including the driver. When it arrived at the Spracklin crossing where the highway turns west a car came from the other side of the track and in the confusion that resulted when each stopped to permit the other to cross the track first, the fact that the southbound passenger was due was entirely overlooked. Just as the Thompson car reached the summit of the grade and was right on the rails the engine of the train struck the car hurling the passengers to instant death or terrible injury.

The women who were riding in the Thompson car were four Modale ladies who had been attending a Kensington at the Thompson home. They were Mrs. Charles Long, Mrs. William Lee, Mrs. Jennie Ross and Mrs. Arthur Hansen. The first two named were instantly killed, Mrs. Ross and Mrs. Hansen were taken to a hospital at Council Bluffs, where Mrs. Ross died shortly after her arrival, and Mrs. Hansen was in such condition that death came Tuesday morning. Thompson, the driver of the car was taken to the hospital also, and he had a leg broken and was otherwise severely bruised and injured.

One of the most tragic things in the horror was the finding of the body of Mrs. Long by her son who was a brakeman on the freight train that came along just after the accident. Brakeman Long helped release the bodies of two women from the pilot of the engine on the passenger train, one of them being Mrs. Ross and the other his own mother.

There has been no satisfactory explanation of the cause of the accident. It was getting dusk, and being a rainy and misty afternoon it is quite likely that the train was not seen nor thought of, and four lives paid the penalty.

Newspapers are the diaries of the communities they serve. Behind the international and national headlines, newspapers tell us about the noteworthy milestones and experiences of our neighbors. Births, deaths, marriages—even divorces—have an impact on the community as well as the family. These events are thus matters of public record and are reported.

For the family historian, microfilmed newspapers in the library can be a shortcut around a trip to the courthouse to examine records. The newspaper will also usually provide more details of the event. This is all relative, of course, to the size of the community being served. In general, the smaller the community, the more information provided.

Newspapers provide other kinds of information as well. Many newspapers, especially in small towns, have society columns that detail local social events. These include dances, engagements, graduations, club and card parties, family gatherings and reunions.

And in some instances, especially with older newspapers, family illnesses, visitors and vacations are reported. Very little was kept secret from the enterprising small town newspaper of yesterday. Although perusing newspapers can be fun and informative, a search can become dauntingly time-consuming without a date to begin with. If possible, search for a newspaper published the day after (or the week after, depending on publication frequency) the event being researched. Generally, the types of articles that will provide the most information about families will be birth, engagement and wedding announcements and, especially, obituaries.

Newspapers
can also be helpful for
researchers checking out clues
provided by the public record. Here is a
routine death certificate of a woman named Mrs.
Long. The death certificate indicated Mrs. Long was
killed in a car-train accident in 1920. A researcher would
check out the local newspaper for an account of the tragedy
that claimed the life of Mrs. Long. The local paper printed not only
Mrs. Long's obituary, but an account of the accident as well. The
story about the accident adds depth, dimension and texture that cannot
be revealed by a simple statement of date of death.

Birth Announcements

Birth announcements will probably offer less family information than the
wedding or death reports. However, some newspapers provide birth news that
includes the hospital, baby's name, weight and length, as well as the parents'
names.

Wedding Announcements

Wedding announcements vary in length and detail. Most big city newspapers will not devote much space to wedding news. The bride, bridegroom and parents are mentioned. Place of residence and employment are also sometimes included. A photograph of the bride is optional.

Smaller newspapers, on the other hand, quite often give detailed information about the wedding as well as the reception. Frequently, the report will include information about the bridal party, the ceremony and, occasionally, even about the bride's dress.

SOCIETY

RASMUSSEN-RIFE NUPTIALS AT CUSTER LAST THURSDAY

Miss Shirley Rasmussen, of Custer, and Wilbur Rife of Lake Andes, were married at Custer April 14 at 4:30 p.m. with Judge D. Webster Davis officiating. The single ring service was used.

The bride chose for her wedding, a powder blue suit and white accessories with which she wore a corsage of red carnations. Her attendant, Miss Margaret Wilhelm, or Hot Springs, was attired in an aqua dress and white accessories. She wore a corsage of pink baby roses.

Andy Thorn of Murdo, attended the groom.

A reception was held at the home of the bride's parents.

Mr. and Mrs. Rife left Friday for Lake Andes, where they will make their home. Rife, who formerly was employed by Peter T. Kiewit and Sons on the Fall River project, is now employed on the Garrison dam project.

Mrs. Rife, until recently, was employed as a waitress at the Cave cafe here.

Obituary

Obituary comes from the Latin word *obitus* meaning "death." An obituary is a newspaper report of someone's death. An obituary usually gives a short sketch of the deceased person's life, including club memberships and religious affiliation, military service, education and professional life. Obituaries also will include the names of the spouse, children, parents, siblings and grandchildren. Obviously, obituaries are a rich source of family history.

Here is the death certificate of Addie Turner. Mrs. Turner died in 1940. The information on the death certificate is helpful, but it is not as complete as the information in an obituary.

Look at Mrs. Turner's obituary and notice the details it provides about her death, her funeral service, her family and her life. Obituaries are short biographies that provide a factual summary of the person's life.

Little information about the deceased appears on the death certificate. Death certificates give only the time, place and direct cause of death. But the death certificate is still very important because it will help you track down the obituary of the dead person.

When you know time, place and cause of death, it becomes a relatively simple matter to check the back files of the community newspaper in which the obituary most likely would have appeared.

Mrs. Addie Turner Dies At Home, Saturday

Funeral services for Mrs. Addie M. Turner were held Tuesday afternoon at two fifteen from the Community church with the Rev. Walter Ross officiating, and burial was in Custer cemetery. Two requested hymns were sung: "Going Down the Valley" and "Rock of Ages," by Mrs. Ross, accompanied at the piano by Mrs. C.E. Perrin. Escorting the body were W.A. Nevin, C.R. Ellerton, Guy Hendrickson, C.E. Rockwell, Henry King and Gus Carlson.

Addie Shepard was born at Missouri Valley, Iowa, Dec. 31, 1865, and died at her home in Custer, June 1 at six o'clock in the morning after having been ill for a day. She suffered a stroke last Friday. She was 74 years and five months old at the time of her passing.

She lived in Iowa until the age of 16. Then with her parents, moved to eastern Nebraska and later to Hay Springs. On Jan. 20, 1884, she was united in marriage to Leon A. Turner, and to this union eight children were born, six of whom are still living.

Eleven years ago the family moved to Custer county, settling on a ranch west of Custer where they lived until the death of Mr. Turner two years ago, and soon after Mrs. Turner came to Custer where she had since lived.

Mrs. Turner was a member of the Latter Day Saints church, a kind and loving mother and a friend to all who knew her.

She leaves to mourn her death, her four sons and two daughters, Mrs. Julia Tisdale of Otis, Colo., Walter Turner of DeNova, Colo., Ray V. Turner of Nevada, Missouri, Mrs. Carrie Rasmussen of Custer, Charles H. Turner of Portland, Ore., Leon A. Turner of Farnum, Nebr., 22 grandchildren, four great grandchildren, two sisters, three brothers, besides other relatives and a host of friends.

Name____

The 5 Ws and the H

Exercise

In a journalistic style—that is, making sure you answer who, what, where, when, how and why—write a birth announcement for yourself. Who are your parents? Who are you? When were you born? Then, using the same journalistic style, write a wedding announcement and an obituary.

Military Service

Word List

bounty land: an award of land for service in the military, awarded only to soldiers who served before 1856

muster out: discharge from military service

muster roll: a roster or inventory of personnel in a military unit

Military Service Records

Most families have ancestors who served in at least one of the wars the United States has been engaged in over the past two hundred plus years. The military service records of these individuals hold interest for family historians. Valuable information can be gleaned from the physical descriptions on the enlistment information, bounty claims and the pension records for the soldiers and their widows.

The National Archives hold military service records for the many wars in which the United States has been involved. If you have ancestors who fought in a war more than 75 years ago, you have a good chance of finding their service records in the National Archives. Service records after that time, however, are protected by the Right to Privacy Act and are not open to the public.

National Archives military service records available for public inspection date back to 1775. Fires have damaged or destroyed some service records, but in general, service records are available for those persons who served in the following wars:

Revolutionary War, 1775-1783

Wayne's War, 1790-1795

The Whiskey Rebellion, 1794

The War of 1812, 1812-1815

The Black Hawk War, 1831-1832

The Mexican War, 1846-1848

The Civil War, 1861-1865

The Spanish American War, 1898

The Philippine Insurrection, 1899-1901

World War I, 1917-1918

Generally,
service records include the
person's name, rank and military
unit, as well as hometown and home
state. In addition, the record might show service
history and payroll records.

Sometimes the records include birth date and place of birth.
Many of the records include applications for pensions and
bounty land. (Bounty land was government land the veteran could
claim as a reward for military service.)

Since widows could apply for their deceased husbands' benefits, the files are also filled with certificates, letters and affidavits to prove the soldier's service and the widow's relationship to the soldier.

If you are searching for military records before 1775, two sources are available. One source is the archives of the United Kingdom. The other source is the archives of the state (i.e., the former colony) for which the serviceperson fought.

Wars prior to 1775 in which colonists might have served are these: King William's War, 1690-1697; Queen Anne's War, 1702-1713; and the French and Indian War, 1754-1763. All of these wars took place in the colonies.

Military Records

On the following page is a company pay roll sheet for Private Jacob Yeisley from the War of 1812. Note that the name *Yeisley* is misspelled. Private Yeisley served in Captain William Fisher's Company of Infantry, 71 Regiment Pennsylvania Militia. Although the service records are interesting, they provide only skimpy amounts of information. That is especially true of early records.

 The War of 1812

Exercise 1

Use Jacob Yeisley's company payroll to answer the following questions:

1. When did Jacob Yeisley enlist in the War of 1812? ________________

2. How long did Yeisley serve?

   ____

3. What was Yeisley's rank?

   ____

4. How much was Yeisley paid for his term of service in the War of 1812?

   ____

5. How much of that amount was a travel allowance? ________________

Y | **71** (Hutter's.) | **Pa. Militia.**

Jacob Yeisely

Prt., { Capt. William Fisher's Company of Infantry, 71 Reg't Pennsylvania Militia.

(War of 1812.)

Appears on

Company Pay Roll

for *Sept. 17 to Dec 20*, 181 4.

Roll dated ...... *Not dated*, 181 .

Commencement of service or of this settlement, } *Sept. 17*, 181 4.

Expiration of service or of this settlement, } *Dec. 20*, 181 4.

Term of service charged, 3 months, 3 days.

Pay per month, 8 dollars, ... cents.

Amount of pay, 24 dollars, 77 cents.

Discharged at Phila. } Distance home, } 90 miles.

20 miles per day, 4½ days.

Am't of pay for traveling home, } 1 dollars, 12 cents.

Total amount, 25 dollars, 89 cents.

Remarks : ....

....

....

....

(572)

Ward

Copyist.

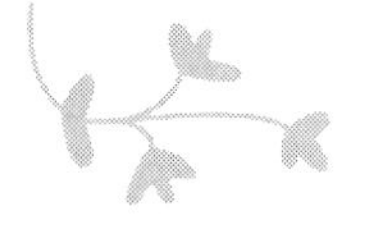
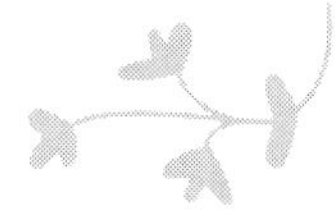

Bounty Lands

READ THESE INSTRUCTIONS CAREFULLY.

This declaration, No. 1, must be signed with the full name, and sworn to before a Justice of the Peace, or other officer authorized to administer oaths in the presence of two witnesses, see affidavit No. 2. Strike out "sold," "located," "or herewith surrendered," according to the fact; if the number of the warrant cannot be remembered, (I can refer to it here,) be sure to give the *number of acres*, the name of the Captain, and the war in which the service was rendered. Insert after the word "company," New York, Pennsylvania, Virginia, or other States—*volunteer* or *militia*, as the fact may be. No warrant can be sold or purchased until issued, when the claimant assigns on the back.

I purchase warrants at the highest prices, when issued, and *properly* assigned.

Respectfully,

WILLIAM HUNT.

FORM FOR BOUNTY LAND UNDER ACT OF 1855.

No. 1. *N°. of former Warrant 5020*

STATE OF *New york* }
COUNTY OF *Chemung* } ss:

On this _*6th*_ day of _*Decemr*_, A. D. one thousand eight hundred and _*fifty five*_, personally appeared before me, a justice of the peace, within and for the county and State aforesaid, _*Jacob Yriesley*_, aged _*Sixty*_ years, a resident of _*Southport Chemung Co*_ in the State of _*New york*_ who, being duly sworn according to law, declares that he is the identical _*Jacob Yriesley*_ who received, under act of 28th September, 1850, a land warrant for _*Forty*_ acres No. _______ for services in Captain _*William Fisher*_ company, _*Regiment of Penna militia*_ war of _*1812*_ which warrant is sold, located, ~~or herewith surrendered~~. *Said Service was rendered at Marcus Hook near Philada the Colonels name not recollected He was drafted at Smithfield Northampton Co in Sep 1814 for three months & was discharged at Marcus Hook in Dec 1814 having servd out his time thinks they were Mustered out of service & recd no other discharge*

He makes this declaration for the purpose of obtaining the Bounty Land, granted by the act passed _*March 3d*_ 1855, and he hereby declares that he has not applied for, or received, and he believes he is not entitled to, Bounty Land except as above stated, and he hereby appoints WILLIAM HUNT, Attorney at Law, of Washington City, D. C., to prosecute his claim, and receive his warrant when issued.*

Signature of claimant ☞ _*Jacob Yriesley*_

Sworn to and subscribed before me, the day and year above written, and I certify that I have no interest in the above claim, and am not concerned in its prosecution.

*Th Maxwell* J. P.
*Chemung Co. N Y*

* If a widow applies, add "that she is now the widow of _______________ and has never married since his death."

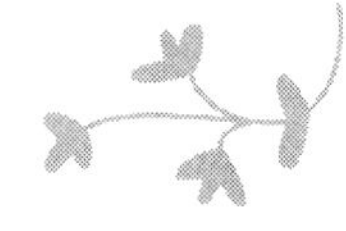

Bounty Lands

On page 130 is a bounty land claim form for Jacob Yeisley. Yeisley served for 95 days in the War of 1812. Under an act passed by Congress in 1855, Jacob Yeisley became eligible to receive bounty land. Giving land to former servicepersons was a way of rewarding veterans for their efforts.

Early in its history, the United States was long on land and short on cash. The first time the United States government gave away land grants was after the Revolutionary War. Those who served from 1776 until the end of the war were awarded land grants. The size of the land grant varied according to the serviceperson's rank.

Veterans could also sell their bounty rights. A cash offer was appealing to many veterans who would rather have the money than move out West where the public domain lands were located.

Exercise 2

Use Jacob Yeisley's bounty land claim form to answer the following questions:

1. Where did Jacob Yeisley live in 1855?

____

2. Had he ever received bounty land before?

____

Pension Records

The first pensions were granted in 1792 to Revolutionary War veterans who had been disabled in combat. Later, any person who had served honorably in the military was eligible for a pension, whether disabled or not.

Exercise 3

Use Jacob Yeisley's pension record at the right to answer the following question:

What amount was Yeisley awarded for a pension? _______________________________________

No. 11,789
—
WAR OF 1812.
—
SURVIVORS' PENSION.

Iowa
Jacob Yeisley
Rank ___________
Company Capt. W'm Fisher
Regiment ___________
Penn'a Militia

Des Moines Agency.
Rate per month— Eight dollars.
Commencing February 14, 1871.

Certificate dated 31st Jan 1872
and sent to Pension Agent.

Act 14th February, 1871.
Vol. Iowa Page 197.
J. M. Kavanaugh Clerk.

Widow's Pension

3—015

DECLARATION FOR WIDOW'S PENSION

Act of May 1, 1920

State of _Nebraska_, County of _Furnas_, ss:

On this _1st_ day of _March_, 192_6_, before me, the undersigned, personally appeared _Lettie Vincent_, who makes the following declaration as an application for pension under the provisions of the act of Congress approved May 1, 1920.

That she is _76_ years of age, that she was born _November 5_, _1849_ at _Warsaw, Indiana_.

That she is the widow of _Hiram G Vincent_, who ENLISTED _November 22_ 1861, at _Magnolia or Calhoun Ia._, under the name of _Hiram G Vincent_, in _Company H - 15th Iowa Volunteer Infantry_ (Here state company and regiment, if in the Army; or vessel, if in the Navy) and was honorably DISCHARGED _June 18_, _1862_, having served ninety days or more, or was discharged for, or died in service of the United States of a disability incurred in the service in the line of duty, during the CIVIL WAR, and who DIED _February 15_, _1926_, at _Cambridge Nebraska_.

That he also served in ___________________ (Here give a complete statement of all other military or naval service, if any, at whatever time rendered)

and that, except as herein stated, said soldier (or sailor) was _not_ employed in the military or naval service of the United States; THAT SHE WAS MARRIED to said soldier (or sailor) _August 20_, _1903_, under the name of _Lettie Ball_, at _McCook, Red Willow Co. Nebr_ by _Rev S Shumak_; that she had _____ been previously married, that he had _____ been previously married; _Jane Buel Vincent first wife of Hiram G Vincent died spring 1902 at Aurora Nebr Lettie Ball divorced from Wesley Ball on March 19, 1900. Certified copy clerk attached._ (If there was a prior marriage of either, the name and the date and place of death or divorce of the former consort, or consorts, should be stated)

That neither she nor said soldier was ever married otherwise than as stated above.

That she was NOT divorced from the soldier (or sailor) and that she has NOT remarried since his death;

That the following are the ONLY children OF THE SOLDIER (or sailor) who are now living and are under sixteen years of age: (If he left no children under sixteen years of age, the claimant should so state)

None under 21 yrs born _____________, 1_____, at _____________

That she _did not_ serve in the Army, Navy, Marine Corps, or Coast Guard of the United States between April 6, 1917, and (Did or did not) July 2, 1921, or at any time during said period.

That _no_ member of her family served in the Army, Navy, Marine Corps, or Coast Guard of the United States between ("a" or "no") April 6, 1917, and July 2, 1921, or at any time during said period. _____________ (If any members of claimant's family were in the military or naval service during the period mentioned, state the full name under which each such member served, with the designation of the organization in (or vessel on) which such service was rendered, together with the dates of enlistment and discharge. State also whether any such members are dead, and if so, give the names)

That she has _not_ heretofore applied for pension, the number of her former claim being _______; that said soldier (or sailor) was _____ a pensioner, the number of his pension certificate being _11824_.

<table>
<tr><td rowspan="6">Two attesting witnesses</td><td>(1) _Emma A Hitton_
(Signature of first witness)</td><td rowspan="3">_Mrs Lettie Vincent_
(Claimant's signature in full)</td></tr>
<tr><td>_Cambridge Nebr_
(Address of first witness)</td></tr>
<tr><td>(2) _Wm Williams_
(Signature of second witness)</td></tr>
<tr><td>_Cambridge Nebr_
(Address of second witness)</td><td>_Cambridge Nebraska_
(Claimant's address in full)</td></tr>
</table>

Subscribed and sworn to before me this _1st_ day of _March_, 192_6_, and I hereby certify that the contents of the above declaration were fully made known and explained to the applicant before swearing, including the words _____________ erased, and the words _____________ added; and that I have no interest, direct or indirect, in the prosecution of this claim.

[L. S.]

B. F. Butler
(Signature)

Notary Public
(Official character)

Cambridge Nebr
(Post office address of officer)

Com exp 10/2/26

O—8411

Widow's Act

In 1836, Congress passed the Widow's Act. This act required the widow of a soldier to submit evidence that she had married her deceased husband prior to the end of the Revolutionary War. This evidence established the widow's claim to a pension. The law was later changed so that by 1854, widows became eligible for pensions regardless of when the couple was married.

Exercise 4

Use Lettie Vincent's declaration for widow's pension on page 132 to answer the following questions:

1. Who was Lettie Vincent? _______________________

2. How old was she? _______________________

3. Whom was she married to before she married Hiram?

   ____

4. Who was Hiram's first wife? _______________________

5. What happened to her?_______________________

6. What happened to Lettie's first husband? _______________

7. When did Lettie marry Hiram? _______________________

8. When did Lettie apply for the pension? _______________

Exercise 5

Use the company descriptive book concerning Hiram Vincent above to answer the following questions:

1. How tall was Hiram Vincent? _______________________

2. How old was he? _______________________

3. Where and when did Hiram Vincent enlist? _______________

4. Why was Hiram Vincent discharged?_______________________

Here is part of the descriptive book of Company H, 15th Regiment of Iowa Infantry. The more recent military service records include more information about the soldiers.

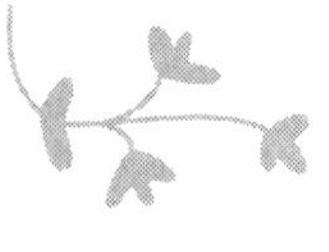
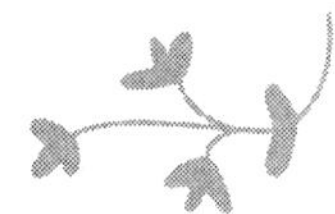

Military Discharge

]

CERTIFICATE OF DISABILITY FOR DISCHARGE.

(To be used, in duplicate, in all cases of discharge on account of disability.)

Hiram G Vincent Corporal of Captain *Clark Co.*
Company, [*H*], of the *Fifteenth (15)* Regiment of United States
Iowa Inft, was enlisted by *Capt. Clark*________________, of
the *Fifteenth* Regiment of *Iowa Inft* at *Calhoun Iowa*
on the *Twenty Second (22)* day of *November* 186*1*, to serve *three* years; he was born
in *Wayne County* in the State of *New York*, is *Twenty one*
years of age, *five (5)* feet *8²* inches high, *Sandy* complexion, *hazel* eyes,
Sandy hair, and by occupation when enlisted a *Farmer*. During the last two
months said soldier has been unfit for duty ______ days. *(Here consult directions on Form 13, p. 325, par. 1340, p. 344, Rev. Army Reg.)*

- -

- -

STATION :

DATE :

Commanding Company.

    I CERTIFY, that I have carefully examined the said *Hiram G Vincent Corporal* of
Captain *Clark's* Company, and find him incapable of performing the duties of a soldier
because of *(Here consult par. 1260, p. 284; also, par. 1638, p. 495, and directions on Form 13, p. 325, Revised Army Regulations)*

Loss of right leg. Amputated below the Knee
result of grape shot wound received at the
battle of Shiloh, Disability three fourths

Jo C Hughes Surgeon
U S Military Hosp

DISCHARGED this *18* day of *June* 186*2* at *St Louis Hosp*

Lieut Munn
Col. Commanding the Post *St Louis Division*

NOTE 1.—When a *probable* case for *pension*, special care must be taken to state the *degree* of disability.
NOTE 2.—The *place* where the *soldier* desires to be *addressed* may be here added.

    Town—   County—   State—

[DUPLICATES.]

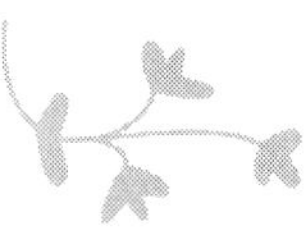
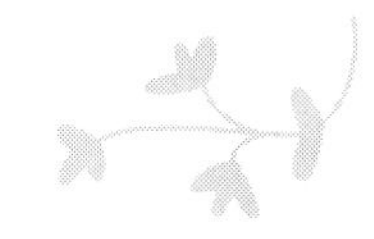

Military Discharge

On page 134 is a discharge certificate. Hiram G. Vincent was discharged for medical reasons.

Exercise 6

Use Hiram Vincent's discharge certificate to answer the following questions:

1. Where was Hiram Vincent born?

   ____

2. What was Hiram Vincent's occupation?

   ____

3. What was Hiram Vincent's military rank?

   ____

4. How was he wounded? _______________________

   ____

5. In what battle was Hiram Vincent wounded?

   ____

6. How much disability pay was he awarded?

   ____

Military Pension

DECLARATION FOR PENSION
Act of May 1, 1920

THE PENSION CERTIFICATE SHOULD NOT BE FORWARDED WITH THE APPLICATION

READ CAREFULLY THE INSTRUCTIONS ON THE REVERSE HEREOF

State of *Nebraska*   County of *Furnas*   ss:

On this *5* day of *December*, 192*5*, before me, the undersigned, personally appeared *Hiram G Vincent*, who makes the following declaration as an application for pension under the provisions of the act of Congress approved May 1, 1920:

That he is *85* years of age; that he was born *Feb 3, 1840* at *Wayne Co. New York*

That he is the identical *Hiram G Vincent* who ENLISTED *Nov 22, 1861* at *Magnolia, Harrison Co. Iowa*, under the name of *Hiram G Vincent* *Co. H. 15th Iowa Inf.*

(Here state company and regiment, if in the Army; if vessel, if in the Navy, and was

DISCHARGED *June 22, 1862* at *Keokuk, Iowa*, having served the United States in the *Civil* War.

(State name of war, Civil or Mexican.

That he also served ____________
(Here give a complete statement of all other military or naval service, if any, at whatever time rendered.)

That otherwise than herein stated he was *Never* employed in the United States military or naval service.

That his personal description at time of first enlistment was as follows: Height *5* feet *8 1/2* inches; complexion *fair*, color of eyes *brown*; color of hair *Sandy*; that his occupation was *farmer*

That since leaving the service he has resided at *Calhoun Ia till 1874 York Co Nebraska till 1890. Oregon 12 yrs. Aurora Nebr 3 yrs. (Cambridge Neb to date)* and his occupation has been *farmer*

That he requires the regular personal aid and attendance of another person and has required such aid and attendance since *Oct. 1, 1925* on account of the following disabilities: *Right leg amputated below knee, result of wound at Pittsburg Landing (Shiloh) April 6, 1862. Double rupture heart trouble, general debility account old age.*

(State in this space the nature of any and all disabilities

That he has ______ applied for pension under Original No. ______; that he is ______ a pensioner under Certificate No. *11824*

(1) *Bessie Cole*,
(Signature of first witness.)
Cambridge, Nebr.
(Address of first witness.)

(2) *George Williams*
(Signature of second witness.)
Cambridge Nebr
(Address of second witness.)

Hiram G Vincent
(Claimant's signature in full.)
Cambridge Nebraska
(Claimant's address in full.)

Subscribed and sworn to before me this *5* day of *December*, 192*5*, and I hereby certify that the contents of the above declaration were fully made known and explained to the applicant before swearing, including the words ______ erased, and the words ______ added; and that I have no interest, direct or indirect, in the prosecution of this claim.

[L. S.]

B.F. Smith
(Signature.)
Notary Public
(Official character.)
Cambridge Nebr
(Post office address of officer.)

6—8172

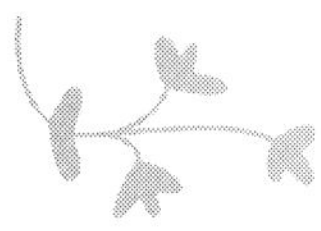

Military Pension

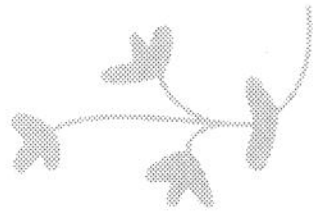

Exercise 7

Use Hiram Vincent's Declaration for Pension to answer the following questions:

1. When was Hiram Vincent born?______________________________________

2. Where was he living when he applied for his pension? _______________

   ____

3. When did he apply? ____

4. How old was he at the time of this application? ____________________

Military
service records often
include even more information
than that presented in this chapter. There
may be lists of children's names, affidavits about
service injuries, a certificate of marriage, records of
children's birth and information about deaths.

Some files, for a variety of reasons, show a great deal more activity than others. Some soldiers did not apply for pensions or bounty lands. Some widows, although eligible, did not apply for their husbands' pensions.

If you want to find out about an ancestor who served in the military, write the Cashier (NJC), National Archives Trust Fund, 8th & Pennsylvania Avenue, N.W., Washington, D.C. 20408, for records. For each record requested, pension, bounty land warrant application (service before 1856 only) or military, the National Archives charges a searching and photocopying fee.

No information will be forthcoming unless your application is completed on a proper form. You can obtain the correct form by writing the National Archives. A basic amount of information is necessary before the National Archives can do your search:

1. Which files do you want searched? __ Pension   __ Bounty Land   __ Military

2. veteran's full name

3. branch of service

4. state from which veteran served

5. war served in, or dates veteran served

6. if service was during Civil War, which army soldier served in

7. unit in which veteran served (name of regiment or number, company, etc., name of ship)

8. if service was Army, specify branch in which veteran served (Infantry, Cavalry, Artillery or other)

9. kind of service (Volunteers, Regulars)

10. pension or bounty land file number

11. date of birth

12. place of birth (city, county, state, etc.)

13. date of death

14. place of death

15. if veteran lived in a home for soldiers, give location

16. place or places veteran lived after service

17. name of widow or other claimant

The National Archives does not have the military service records for World War II. Inquiries about those records should be directed to the following government office:

National Personnel Records
G.S.A. (Military Records)
9700 Page Boulevard
St. Louis, Missouri 63132

You should also be aware that there are restrictions on the release of military service records unless the records are 75 years old or older.

Family History Never Ends

Your students' journey through
this workbook has provided them with
the information and skills to find out more
about themselves. Your students' research also
should have helped them discover more about the
people who make up their families.

Through exercises in this workbook, they have looked into their families' past. They have realized that their families and their experiences are unique. No other family has the same story to tell. This story, rich with detail and history, spans generations and brings young and old together.

The story is continuous, too. Researching family history takes its pursuers on a never-ending journey. New family members, changing family traditions, and fresh discoveries will add more fascinating stages to the journey. Have fun traveling.

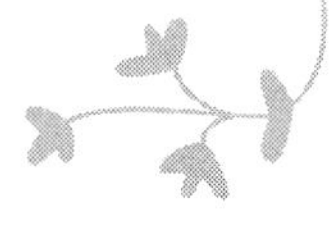

Answer Key

Families, page 12

The drawings that students are asked to do in this section will all be different. The exercise is designed to demonstrate to the class that there is no rigid definition of what makes up a family. When the exercise is completed, you might ask students to compare their drawings with those done by other students and discuss how each student has defined his or her family.

Family Relationships, pages 15-16

This section is designed to help each student understand his or her own place in his or her family's history. In discussing this section with students, you may want to reinforce the idea that the history of each student's family can affect the way he or she looks and acts today.

Pedigree, pages 20-23

Students will probably be required to gather some information from their parents and other family members in order to complete the exercises in this section. If desired, the material in the following two sections can be discussed in class while students gather this information at home.

In addition to the pedigree charts presented in this section, a different type of chart called a radial pedigree chart is sometimes used by family historians. An example of a radial chart appears on page 22.

Family Records, pages 25 and 31

Each family has an archive of sorts filled with documents that can be used to piece together the past. You may want to point out to students that along with Bible entries and funeral programs, the family historian can draw from diplomas, samplers and quilts, initialed and engraved flatware and account books for information about a particular family.

In addition, library resources can tell a lot about families. Histories of cities and counties can often be found in city and county libraries. Family information is often included in these histories. Also, many libraries have copies of old city directories. These directories list the place of residence and business of most people living in a city at a particular time. This can help the family historian determine when someone moved to and left a particular place.

Photographs, page 36

Exercise

1. This couple was recently married and are wearing their very best—fancy shoes and clothes—and their new wedding bands.

2. Students should note that not only does the younger boy wear a dress, but they both wear stockings and bows. The younger boy's hair has been allowed to grow long while the older boy's has been cut short.

3. Men: hats, top button buttoned on coat, button shoes, large pant cuffs

   Women: hats, gloves, bow, shoes (students may discover more differences)

Note: To emphasize the value of photographs to family history, you may want to have students bring some of their own family photographs to class. Students could then discuss the similarities and differences between various photographs.

Oral History, page 45

Be sure to allow students to share their recorded interviews or transcripts with the class.

The Internet, page 46

When students discover helpful new genealogy web sites online (the numbers grow every day), make certain they share the addresses and information with the rest of the class.

Religious Records, page 50

Exercise 1

1. b; 2. e; 3. d; 4. c; 5. a; 6. a; 7. f

Exercise 2

1. An established church is a church designated by the ruler of a country to be an official state church. Historically, this meant that all of the people in a country that had an established church were supposed to belong to that church.

2. The Council of Trent

3. Baptism, marriage and burial records can be found in a church or synagogue.

4. The First Amendment to the Constitution guarantees freedom of religion in America.

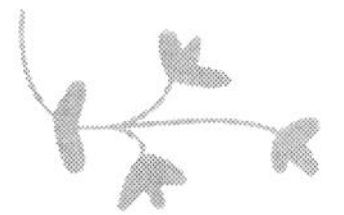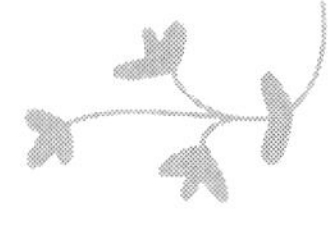

Answer Key

Diaries & Journals, pages 56-64

Exercise 1

Students' definitions will vary, but the following are possible responses:

goose hung high—everyone was having a good time.

jolly boy—a fun person.

chivalree—a raucous party after a wedding.

bones player—musician, possibly a trombone player or one who plays wooden clappers to keep in time with the music.

gay time—a fun time, a good time.

serenading—singing or playing an instrument to gain the favor of a sweetheart.

Note: Students should be aware that there are other personal family documents besides diaries and journals that have great historical worth. Letters, for example, can be very valuable to the family historian.

Cemeteries

Exercise 2, page 72

1. Symbolism is the use of certain symbols or images to stand for or represent something else. On gravestones, symbols are used to represent spiritual and intangible things. For instance, a gravestone relief sculpture of a dove to portray the Holy Spirit represents religious symbolism. An intangible quality like strength is represented by an oak leaf.

2. Cemeteries are important to family historians because they record the past. They are a rich source of vital statistics and reveal a great deal about the lives and deaths of people.

3. Generally, gravestones can provide information on names, birth and death dates and information on whether or not a person has served in the military. Gravestones also display the art and symbolism of death, which can provide insight into the lives of the deceased.

Exercise 3, page 72

1. e; 2. c; 3. h; 4. d; 5. f; 6. b; 7. g; 8. a

Exercise 4, page 75

1. Epitaphs are inscriptions on gravestones and tombs marking the memory of a dead person.

2. Epitaphs are sometimes written by a family member or friend of the deceased, pulled from an epitaph book or composed by the deceased before death.

3. Any two of the following may be mentioned: epitaph books, writings of family members, personal writings, the Bible.

Note: The demonstration of the techniques of gravestone rubbing is an important part of this section. You may ask students to bring their gravestone rubbings to class to analyze the symbolism and imagery of the stones that they rubbed.

Census Records, page 95

Exercise 1

1. A census is a counting of people and property.

2. The census is taken every 10 years in the United States.

3. The U.S. Constitution ordered a census so that the results of the census could be used as a basis for determining the number of representatives each state would have in the Congress.

4. The *Domesday Book* is the result of a census ordered by William the Conqueror in 1085. The book lists the names of English people, along with their possessions.

5. The census of 1850 is the early census that is likely to be most helpful to family historians.

6. The 1890 census was almost completely destroyed by a fire in Washington, D.C.

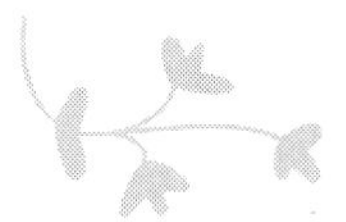

Answer Key

7. A special census ordered by Congress in 1890 counted Civil War Union veterans. That census could be useful because it lists each veteran's rank, company, regiment, or vessel. It also lists the veteran's date of enlistment, discharge, length of service, postal address, and, if the veteran was deceased, it lists his surviving spouse.

8. A mortality schedule is a record of those who have died during a specific time period.

Note: In order to provide students with hands-on experience with census records, you may want to try to obtain some actual records and have the students examine them in class. Students could be asked to try to determine the time period of the census from the type of information included on the census form.

Immigration, pages 97-98

Stories of immigration can be fascinating. Students from immigrant families might be asked to tell the story of their family's immigration in class.

Maps

Exercise 2, page 103
1.e; 2. d; 3. a; 4. c; 5. b

Exercise 3, page 104
1. b; 2. c; 3. b; 4. d; 5. c; 6. a

Note: As an in-class activity, you might provide students with different historical maps of their city, county or state, showing them how the boundaries of these areas have changed over time.

Wills, page 110

Exercise 1

1. Ezra Vincent is the testator of the will.

2. Jonathan Vincent and S.T. Hardy served as executors.

3. S.T. Hardy is Ezra Vincent's son-in-law.

4. H.H. Roadifer and N.B. Hardy were witnesses to the signing of the will.

5. Ezra Vincent left one bed, one bureau, one horse and one thousand dollars ($1000) to his daughter Viola.

6. Answers will vary, but following is just one example of how wills, by listing the heirs, can help the family historian: Daughter Viola was married to S.T. Hardy. And, although we don't know who Emma and Julia married, we do have a starting point. The will lists these two daughters by their married names. Those married names give a clue as to who to look for when searching for their families.

Note: After students have completed writing their own wills in Exercise 2, you may want to ask them to analyze their wills in terms of their value to future family historians. What could each will tell you about its author and his or her family?

Vital Statistics, page 121

Exercise 1

1. Vital statistics are records of such events as births, marriages and deaths.

2. Yes, vital statistic records are considered primary information sources for research.

3. Because of the difference in centralized record keeping practices between the states, it is important to have copies of the U.S. government's pamphlets to guide you to the right place.

Note: Students should be aware that divorce records are also an important source of information. The government publishes a pamphlet called *Where to Write for Divorce Records: United States and Outlying Areas*. This publication is available from the U.S. Government Printing Office, Superintendent of Documents, Washington, D.C. 20402. When writing to request divorce records, you should include as much of the following information as possible:

1. Full names of husband and wife (including nicknames)

2. Their current place of residence, if living

3. Former addresses

4. Ages at the time of the divorce (or dates of birth)

5. Date (month, day and year) of the divorce or annulment

6. Place of divorce or annulment

7. Type of final decree

8. Purpose for which copy is needed

9. Your relationship to persons whose record is being requested

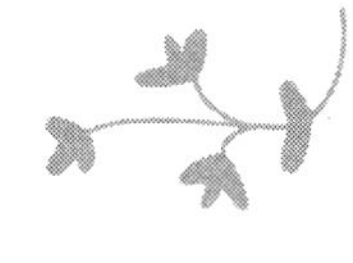

Answer Key

Students should also know that vital statistics can be obtained from the library of the Church of Jesus Christ of Latter Day Saints in Salt Lake City, Utah. (This library is mentioned as a source of church records in the section "Religious Records," and a source of census records in the section "Census Records.") Information about Mormon collections of family records can be obtained by writing The Genealogical Department, Church of Jesus Christ of Latter-Day Saints, 50 East North Temple Street, Salt Lake City, Utah 84150.

Newspapers, page 126

As an exercise in using newspapers for family history research, students could be asked to examine their local newspapers for a week, clipping birth announcements, wedding announcements, obituaries and other articles of interest to the family historian. Students could then compare their clippings and discuss the value of what they have found.

Military Service

Exercise 1, page 129

1. Jacob Yeisley enlisted in the War of 1812 on September 17, 1814.

2. Yeisley served for three months and three days.

3. Yeisley's rank was private.

4. Yeisley was paid $25.89 for his term of service in the War of 1812.

5. Of that amount, $1.12 was a travel allowance.

Exercise 2, page 131

1. Jacob Yeisley lived in Southport, Chimung County, New York, in 1855.

2. Yes, he received 40 acres of bounty land under an act of 28th September, 1850.

Exercise 3, page 131

1. Yeisley was awarded $8.00 per month for a pension.

Exercise 4, page 133

1. Lettie Vincent was the widow of Hiram Vincent, a Civil War soldier.

2. She was 76 years old.

3. She was married to Wesley Ball before she married Hiram.

4. Jane Buel Vincent was Hiram's first wife.

5. She died in Aurora, Nebraska, in the spring of 1902.

6. Lettie divorced her first husband on March 19, 1900.

7. Lettie married Hiram on August 20, 1903.

8. Lettie applied for the pension on March 1, 1926.

Exercise 5, page 133

1. Hiram Vincent was five feet, eight and a half inches, tall.

2. He was 21 years old.

3. Hiram Vincent enlisted on November 22, 1861, at Calhoun.

4. Hiram Vincent was discharged because he was severely wounded in the leg at the Battle of Shiloh. His leg was amputated.

Exercise 6, page 135

1. Hiram Vincent was born in Wayne County, New York.

2. Hiram Vincent's occupation was farmer.

3. Hiram Vincent's military rank was corporal.

4. He was wounded by grape shot and had his right leg amputated below the knee.

5. Hiram Vincent was wounded in the Battle of Shiloh.

6. He was awarded three-fourths disability pay.

Exercise 7, page 137

1. Hiram Vincent was born on February 3, 1840.

2. He was living in Cambridge, Nebraska, when he applied for his pension.

3. He applied on December 5, 1925.

4. He was 85 at the time of this application.

Note: Military service records and other records can be fascinating sources of family history. If any student have these types of records at home, they might be asked to bring them to class and compare them with the records found in this section.